MW01384860

Really Really Terrible Girls

By Jennifer Barnick

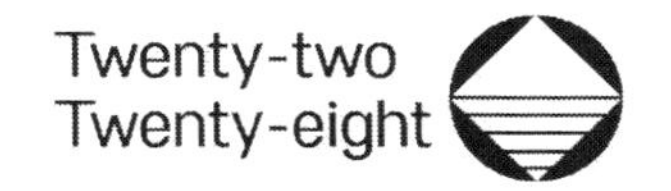

Twenty-two Twenty-eight
Medford, MA
twentytwotwentyeight.com

Printed in the United States
Published in 2017 by Twenty-two Twenty-eight
First Edition

ISBN: 978-0-9991010-0-1 (paperback)
ISBN: 978-0-9991010-1-8 (ebook)

Library of Congress Control Number: 2017909246

Check us out at:
twentytwotwentyeight.com
Or follow us on Facebook at Twenty-two Twenty-eight

To Tim and Rose

Table of Contents

Violence

Peter Peter
(Emma)

He just hated her. He hated her with a span and depth that made his chest swell; his heart would sink and then collapse when he saw her laugh or talk or walk ahead of him. Her hips had a way. Her hips would not just sway as they should just sway; rather, they would roll in an uneven waterly way like a bucket too full and sloshing. Her mouth formed words as though they were first smiles or smirks. He would just cringe when she told people about her day, and even words like *then* and *other* and *microphone* (which normally were very steady white sheet words) would sound a little odd or maybe mysterious or perhaps hysterical when she said them. She could make going to the drug store to purchase some chewing gum and some pantyhose and a magazine sound like it was a trip to Lisbon, and everyone in Lisbon suddenly started to act like people from Berlin, and well, this really got to him. Every description that came out of her disorientating teeth made the world sound upside down and a little wobbly. He would very often catch himself not breathing when she talked; he always felt very uncomfortable when he was not breathing. Oh, and her laugh, he would spend entire commutes home simply bemoaning her laugh. It was the worst sound in the world, and as if the universe was punishing him in the most personal and provocative way, she laughed more than she talked or walked ahead of him. Naturally regarding the walking ahead of him, because every time they were *trying* to walk somewhere, she was admiring a front door or an old lady dressed smartly, and there was also her left shoe slipping off or gum on her shoe or a penny to be picked up or a dropped cookie. There was always something stopping her, snagging her, slowing her, and these snags were always terribly lame. How is a dog peeing on a fire hydrant funny? Why is carrying a large musical instrument lovely? How could anybody be so lame? And walking ahead of him, talking, and laughing were only three things he hated about her. There were actually thousands of things he hated about her.

There were some things, though they rarely happened, where his sense of revulsion was so intense he actually thought of harming her. No, not to really kill her but to hit her. No, not to really hit her but to maybe stab her with a stiff, offended pointer finger. No, not to really stab her with a stiff, offended pointer finger but to simulate without actually touching her strangulation. No, not to really simulate without actually touching her strangulation but to really really glare at her. He would really really glare at her when she took off into a river for absolutely no reason. She did this once when they were on a drive through the country. It was in the afternoon, and he was driving them to a friend's house that was out in the country. His friends were throwing a party for their son's first birthday, so there was some importance to the trip. She asked him with notes of urgency to pull over to the side of the road. Thinking something bad was about to happen that perhaps might be less bad if she were not in the car, he quickly pulled over. She then darted out of the car and trotted straight into a modest river that had been running parallel to the country highway. As she pulled off her sandals while still skipping towards the water, he yelled at her to come back. He then yelled that they were running late, but she ignored him as she waded around the river, getting her sundress soaked right up to her waist. When she returned, he was furious, and worse still, her dress was getting his car seat wet. He really really glared at her and asked her why she would do something like that, and she just laughed. On another occasion, he was showing her a rose quartz crystal skull he had purchased in Lima, Peru from an ancient witch who had read him his fortune. As he was showing her his crystal skull and telling her about his fortune telling experience and what he thought about it, she picked it up and ran off with it and kept rolling it all over his house like a bowling ball. He was not only angry but hurt. She, however, thought it was the funniest thing in the world. Luckily, he also felt a little smug, as the fortune teller in Lima, who out of absolute desperation he consulted because of her and her torturous ways, warned him that she might do the exact sort of thing she did when espying his rose quartz crystal skull. So, while he was angry and hurt that she was rolling his treasure all over his house (*and really scaring his cats Pepper and Piper*) (for which she refused to call by their names and would call them *Butthole* and *Licker*) he did have the sense of calm or maybe even power knowing that this was exactly what he knew she would do with his crystal skull from Lima, Peru. Once he finally got the skull back from her, again he really really glared at her.

Some of the things he hated about her messed him up inside, because he knew these were things he used to like. He used to like it when someone complimented him on what he was wearing. She had irrecoverably destroyed that little human pleasure. In fact, she had turned it into a terrifying moment of extreme self-doubt along with suspicions of revenge. She was repotting a plant in the kitchen when he walked into the kitchen all ready to go to work. She then set her trowel down, took off her flowered gloves, put the spilling plant stuff on the counter, turned to him, looked at him right in the eyes and said, "I like what you are wearing." He just cringed and then wanted to burn the outfit. He also used to like when someone would loan him something he needed to borrow. It was such a pleasant human operation. Because of her, he was now absolutely terrified to ask to borrow something. When he would ask to borrow her sewing scissors, she would hand him a pair of regular scissors; when he would ask to borrow her dictionary, she would hand him her old, over-abridged, college dictionary. And when he would press her on these missed marks, she would sigh heavily and get her sewing scissors and complete, hardcover dictionary.

For the most part, he was relatively gentlemanly regarding his hatred towards her. However, there were a few notable times when he did explode, and to be honest, besides the actual original event that provoked him, her reaction to his explosions stirred a second, defeated hatred. One time, she simply could not pick a restaurant. They were downtown and starved, and all she could do was read the posted menu outside and bite her lower lip and move on to the next boxed and lit-up menu. After around the seventh or eighth restaurant, he finally lost it. He called her a fucking crazy bitch and walked aggressively towards her. She turned and proceeded to walk briskly ahead of him as he followed her closely behind and yelled at her. He did stop briefly to purchase some Mexican take-out but managed to catch up with her easily, and in between bites of his burrito, he would swear at her. When they got back to her apartment, she told him that he had to go back to his house and that he was not going to stay at her place. He then threw the rest of his burrito at her and left. Well, he did not *really* leave. He sat in the hallway and leaned against the door while periodically (according to his energy levels that did wax and wane, for it was a rough night, and he was still quite hungry, and he had left his dinner inside of her apartment) bang her apartment door with his head. On another occasion, she just was not dressed hippie enough. He was a big fan of the Burning Man experience. He came with plenty of tie-dye t-shirts and nylon-strapped sandals. She showed up wearing a pair of cut-offs and a black silk top with little white flowers and a pair of black ballet flats, and this set him off, because she really stood out, and a lot of people were looking at her. So as they were putting up their blue tent, he simply boiled over in the desert heat (he would later remind himself on many evenings that the heat is rather strong in Nevada). He asked her very loudly why on earth she thought to wear such an outfit to *Burning Man* and that she absolutely did not fit in and that he was completely embarrassed to be seen with her. In fact, he was so offended by her outfit that he wasn't even sure that he could bear her presence himself, alone with her in the tent. She turned and walked off, but before she was completely out of sight, she purchased a can of beer from some old hippie couple dressed like George Washington and Marilyn Monroe. He tried to follow her but was unable as she was swept away by a jolly singing group of ten or so naked young men. They had put a wreath of flowers on her head before they gently drew her into their fold. She was laughing, and really, he knew he probably *could* run over to them and get her back, but she looked so lame with the completely embarrassing wreath of flowers on her head (and not to mention her ugly laugh) that he just hung out by the blue tent. She returned late in the evening swaying in a light cool breeze kind of way as she was coming gracefully down from a magic mushroom that was given to her by her gallant footmen. They told her that she was their queen; however, for her to actually see her kingdom, she must ingest *the portal.* She was laughing hysterically as they were explaining all of this to her. Many of the men had tied pretty little things like flowers, brass bells, and colored ribbons around their penises.

As his hatred grew in both intensity and variety, he knew he had to do something to mitigate the extraordinary pressure. So, he decided to record and catalog his many hatreds. He would write them down at the end of every day, making a special note of a newly discovered thing he hated about her or of a hate that was really beginning to grow in its hatiness. He had gone to an old style stationary store and purchased bookkeeping ledgers with numbered pages. The pages were numbered, so he could know if any of the pages were torn away. In no time at all, he would have to put up another shelf to make room for his hate ledgers. After a while, he would have to move his desk and printer and other office furniture into the guest room of his house to accommodate the rows and rows of ledgers. He always felt a notable rise in peace and control when he would walk in his hate-her room and put his daily recorded hates up on a shelf. They would be exactly where he left them when he would return the next evening to again record the day's hates and again make a special note of any newly found hates and of the previously moderate things he hated about her that were becoming quite hot.

Much to his surprise and irritation, she seemed to enjoy the hate books nearly as much as he did. She would curl around him while he was recording the day's hates, wearing no underwear and a cotton t-shirt that always said just awful things like: 'I love myself' (with the comic character Garfield kissing his paw) or 'Texas.' Later she became even crueler and would do things like offer suggestions and remind him of things she had done that annoyed him. But what finally killed every bit of joy and happiness he received from his nightly bookkeeping was when he discovered that she not only had been going through and reading his many hate books that lined all of the wall space in his old office, but she had also begun writing in them. With a red pen, she would not only correct his grammar but later offer more profound suggestions regarding style. When he confronted her with this, she first briefly tried to defend her editorial prowess, but only half-heartedly, because, for the most part, she was laughing so hard that she could barely speak. And to make matters worse, she was wearing one of her worst t-shirts yet—it was light yellow and written in navy blue across her chest were the words 'tennis balls.' And again, she was without any underwear. "Really what kind of insane person rolls around on the carpet laughing and wearing a t-shirt that simply says 'tennis balls' and thinks it is utterly okay not to wear underwear? He wore his underwear all of the time. It was a perfectly natural and comfortable thing to do; why could she not understand that human dignity—underwear?" he thought to himself while holding in an angry, spilling way several opened hate books that had been pretty heavily marked over with red ink.

He naturally had to take all of his hate books and dump them in the bay. It felt like such a relief and such a complete loss. Something just had to be done. He hated her so much. He drove around the city for several hours crying out of agony, self-pity, and seething, complete, whole-hearted hatred. His heart and mind were so riotously loud that when he finally pulled up to his house, he felt crooked walking to his front door in the silent serenity of first dawn.

The house was completely quiet and just beginning to receive dawn's light. Even Pepper and Piper were sleeping. He walked into his kitchen and sat down at the table, and under only the subtlest sheets of rising light, he put his head in his hands. With an uncanny and remarkable speed, dawn gave way to morning, and his house, though not bright, was lit up in a sad, utterly visible within the gray sort of way. Even Pepper and Piper were stirring. The day had come. He first took off his running shoes and then made coffee, and as the coffee hissed and dripped, he fed begging and rubbing Pepper and Piper. He returned to the table and resumed holding his head. Only when the coffee began to burn on the heat plate of the coffee maker did he think to have a cup of coffee. He drank nearly the whole burnt pot and was relieved that for once something tasted like it should under the circumstance. That was another thing that he hated about her—she never really acted in the right way one should under the circumstance.

After finishing his bitter though appropriate coffee, he rose and walked to his bedroom. That part of the house was still quite dark and utterly silent. The sandpaper sound from the rubbing seams of his jeans seemed incredibly loud as he walked down the last turn of the hallway that led to the master bedroom. He stood outside the bedroom door for some time before he turned the knob. There she was sound asleep. She was curled loosely on her side with the blankets pinned between her knees. In the sparse and uneven light, her exposed bare leg looked like it had been chopped off and placed on top of the bed instead of being connected to a live human. Her slim hands were clasped together and tucked under her cheek. Her breathing was steady though barely visible. He sat on his side of the bed and proceeded to take off all of his clothes except for his underwear and crawled into bed. He wanted desperately to fall asleep but could not. He then leaned over and touched her shoulder. At first, it was cool cotton, but then as he held his fingers against her t-shirt covered shoulder, her life first warmed then heated. He then gently pulled her shoulder down to make her upper body roll naturally. He then did the same with her knees. She was a sound asleep butterfly.

He loved her so terribly. There seemed to be no end to all of the things he loved about her. Her hair, too soft to be human and yet profoundly human in its softness, always had a mysterious way of smelling like hope and peace, for when his face was buried in her hair, he felt as if he was capable of anything. He loved the way her hands hung limp though lively at her sides when she waited in line for popcorn at the movies or for a ticket to ride the merry-go-round or to renew her parking permit. Everyone else around seemed to have grotesque meat-chop hands that almost appeared to be grabbing the air or spidery hands that crept and crawled all over scratching and adjusting and touching. His loves for her would rise to such an intensity that he would feel as though someone should tie him down, lock him up. His love for her would at times press so painfully against his skin from the inside that he wished he could slash himself for the relief of pressure. After reading and re-reading one of her infrequent, though wit-alighted emails, he would often have to find an empty conference room at work and try to call her. She was unable to pick up her phone at work, and he knew that. However, calling her and leaving a message managed a little relief of the pressure of his intense and unyielding love. Every once in a while, she would answer, and when this happened, his heart pounded. Always whether it was simply a message left or a brief live exchange afterward, he would for a fleeting bolt come apart. He would then rub his face with his hands and return to his desk.

There were simply so many things he loved about her, and sometimes he would sit in his car and marvel at the fact. When he did this either at his work's underground parking garage or in front of his house, he would cry a great deal. She did catch him once as she was leaving to attend a friend's baby shower. She was holding an enormous stuffed panda and a bottle of wine. She tapped the driver's side window of his car with the black foiled head of the bottle. Embarrassed, he lowered his window. She asked him what was wrong, and he told her *nothing*. She then asked if he was sure, and he said that he was sure. She then frowned; however, she was holding a giant stuffed panda and a bottle of wine. She had to go.

And there she was, this lovely sleeping butterfly. He stared intently at her. There was a halo-shaped, blurred ring of light surrounding the shaded window above the headboard and just lightly, like the finest baby powder imaginable, a dusting of light lit her face and body. She glowed. He went to touch her thigh but paused and then ran his hand all over her body from her forehead to her feet without actually lowering his hand low enough to touch her. Even without actually touching her, he could feel her life and heat radiate and warm and tickle the face of his hand. He then leaned over to kiss her, but like his hand, he stayed himself and chose to run his face over her as he did with his hand beginning from her forehead to her feet. Her smell was impossible to him; impossible in that it stirred his love and hate for her so powerfully that his brain and body felt as though they were being overrun, outdone, inverted, and yet, swelled. He rolled back to the edge of his side of the bed and tried to sleep curled with his back to her. This, of course, was impossible.

He could cry though. He wept and wept. The tears were no longer drops, rather, smooth veins. His body trembled and shook as he cried and cried. His pillow was soaked all around and underneath his heavy, curled face. This woman had completely ruined him, and he knew it, saw it. He remembered his friends from work and how before her they would often go out drinking together, and life was light and fun. He could still perfectly see his friends' faces laughing and sometimes grimacing in deep trouble as he remembered there was a time when friends would come to him with a problem, and they would drink beers and toss his old basketball into his old basketball hoop on his driveway. He thought of the day he bought the hoop. There were even girls over to help commemorate what was touted to be the most genius home improvement act *ever*. The day was sunny, and at first, it was just him and his used-to-be-but-now-never-see best buddy. They drove to a large mega mart and picked it out. They then went to a large mega-liquor mart for a keg and the workings for shots and some white wine for the hoped-for girls.

There were so many things that he desperately missed and lost because of her. He used to be so caring—everyone would say that to him and about him to others. If someone was having a hard time at work, like say with a computer or cell phone, he was the first to help. If someone's car was at the repair shop, he was the first one to offer to give a ride. And he once even drove a co-worker to the hospital after she had thought she had broken her fingers in the heavy, fire-proof door that lead to the building's stairway. And his parents, he used to call them all the time and at least once a quarter do the six-hour drive and visit them. Likewise, they too would try to come up once a quarter. Since her, however, they have been too busy to visit, and he knew the real reason, and that was that they could not stand her—though mainly because of what was happening to their son and not any particular character fault she possessed. Likewise, he stopped driving down, because he could not stand leaving her alone, away from him.

And he used to have interests. He wept and thought of a time, the time before *her*, and how he used to do things. He would sometimes take a course at the Museum of Fine Art like 'Death and Fruit in Paint' and 'Syphilis.' He actually sometimes played the guitar, and he used to go check out new bands downtown. Sometimes he would go with friends, and sometimes he would even go alone and deeply enjoy the romantic gesture of going to a show alone. Now, of course, he did not even listen to music in his car, for he needed that precious time to think of her.

Oddly enough, it was that very last thought, the fact that he did not even listen to his car stereo anymore because he was so completely occupied with her, that his tears and soggy spirit began to quickly dry up. "There has to be an end to this agony," he thought.

A familiar, yet nonetheless startling softness brushed across his face. He rolled onto his back and looked into her gazing eyes. She was leaning over him, and her hair was framing his cry pocked face. "What is wrong?" she asked.

"I can't take it anymore," he said weakly.

She held her gaze for some time. His heart pounded as he wanted to embrace her, pitch her off the bed, and run away. She then sighed and lifted her head from its hover over his. She then began to slide off the bed but stopped, because he had grabbed her left forearm extremely firmly.

"What is this going to do?" she asked while looking down on her forearm and his shaking hold, for he was holding her arm so tightly that his hand, wrist, and forearm were shaking.

"The agony just has to end. I can't take it anymore," he pleaded.

"Look! It's Butthole and Licker!" she yelled. The two cats had come bounding in, for they were chasing each other.

Caught off guard by the surprising interruption, he briefly let go of his grip and turned to see the cats. She immediately jumped off the bed and ran. He too jumped off the bed and took off after her. The flight through the house after her was the most wondrous thing he had ever experienced in his entire life. He could see her frantically undoing all of the locks on the door in the laundry room that led to the garage where her car was parked. He slowed his pace to a walk simply to extend and savor the moment. She finally freed the door and ran to her car. He ran after her. While she was starting her car, he ran to jam the garage door (which was already beginning to slowly creak open) by shoving a slim tack hammer into one of the many slots of the door's side rail around a foot and a half above the ground. He then grabbed a shovel and proceeded to slam its rusty, heavy head against her windshield. She was crying heavily and shaking a great deal. He then walked around to the driver's side and began to slam both the driver's side window and the roof of her white BMW.

The car's engine roared as she put it in reverse and pushed her foot down all the way to the floor of her car. And like the final lunar capsule leaving behind its too heavy rocket base, the car burst through the garage door hurting but not so much to not scream away. He dropped the shovel and simply gawked at his surroundings.

Slowly, he not only returned his home to its

previously wholesome condition, he also returned to his friends and his life of lightness and interest in activities like taking classes at the Museum of Fine Art, and indeed he did take a class there called 'Life in Ink.' It was in his class where he met her, and she would become his wife. And as he neared his parent's house, he gazed down peacefully at his wife who had a pumpkin pie resting on her lap, for it was Thanksgiving. And really there were so many things he felt grateful for. *Thousands really.*

He was especially grateful for his wife and all her many ways. When she came over for the first time, he introduced his beloved Pepper and Piper to her, and from there on out, she called them *Pepper* and *Piper*. And when he once asked if she could hand him the tongs, for he was about to grill them some steaks, she walked to the kitchen drawer where the tongs were, pulled out the tongs, and then handed them to him. Once, he was a little nervous, as he had to do a presentation to a fairly large group at work, and he asked her how he looked, and she said, *great*. Burning Man was finally enjoyable again, as she too packed plenty of tie dye t-shirts and a pair of nylon-strapped sandals—in fact, she allowed him to buy them and pack them for her, because she said she had no idea how to dress for Burning Man. He was just so grateful for her. So absolutely grateful, for rarely did she walk ahead of him or behind him being held up by a lost dog poster or a cozy old man. She always walked at his side and almost never noticed anything lovely or funny. And finally, to sleep with a woman that was not in any way impossible to hold. Her hair smelled just like shampoo and felt like his, and her body was female. Not Butterfly. He was truly utterly grateful for his new wife whom he met in class at the museum—not on accident as he had with *her*. Meeting a girl in a class at a museum was so much better than bending over a crying girl who had just wiped out on her bicycle and was bleeding on her palms, knees, and chin. And while his and his wife's first encounter was over coffee at the museum café, his with the *other one* was in the bathroom of her extremely messy apartment blowing on her injuries to lessen the pain in between shriek-worthy dabs of hydrogen peroxide.

However, those were just the little things he was so utterly grateful for regarding his new wife. What he was the most grateful of all for was the fact that he did not hate his new wife. Not ever, and it was such a relief to feel like a human being again and not some monster. He absolutely would not be dedicating whole rooms to hate ledgers. Lastly, the most profound thing of all he was grateful for was that he did not achingly love his new wife. He would say that he *loved her*, but the love that she invoked was rather like popcorn or peanuts. Surely, she would never catch him crying in his car in front of their house.

There really was only one thing that did continue to haunt him regarding *the one that he hated*, and that was their final moments together, and really nothing would ever be as completely gripping and true and life-filled as his last explosive dance with her. Every so often, he would allow himself the indulgence of playing the whole scene over in his head. Sometimes he would start with her at the laundry room door, sometimes he would start with him dumping the hundreds of hate books into the bay, and sometimes he would start with him running his face over her sleeping body under the morning's powdery glow. When he did allow himself to run back over that last time with *her*, his whole body would pump electric, and for the tiniest teeniest moment he would do anything in the world to find her again and pull her as hard as he could back into his life and blue tent and master bedroom.

Before he and his wife climbed out of the car, he asked if she would pause for just a moment. She paused. He looked down at the pink box tied with white butcher's string on her lap. He had asked her to pick up a pumpkin pie for Thanksgiving, and that was exactly what she did. She even purchased it from the precise bakery he had requested. And with a sense of couch calm, he leaned over and kissed her on the cheek.

The Shack
(Beth)

The house had been inherited by his wife and was a large, art-filled *shack*. The house was designed and built by an architect of some renown along with his wife's father and uncle. Their intention was to make a house appear and feel as though one was residing in a shack without all the peril and nuisance of actually having to live in a real shack.

On several nights he had pressed his wife and her siblings regarding what was actually meant by *shack*, and usually the response was something like: "Well, a shack is a crude residence or shelter made by a person without the means to properly build a home." This definition was never fully satisfying, as it still left him completely mystified as to why on earth would somebody build not only a proper house but a house of some size and luxury out in very tony bramble country with the intention of having it emulate a shack—a crude shelter possibly built by a transient or fleeing criminal?

The response whether from his wife as she was taking off her clothes for bed or from his brother-in-law as he was shooting wine bottles with an anemic rifle behind *the shack* was: "A shack is more appropriate for a human than a house. However, because my family over generations had collected many valuable things, it seemed that we indeed needed a house. Luckily, my father and his architect friend came up with the best possible solution." Again, this always made him feel extremely uneasy, as it seemed to him a kind of pretense on the part of his wife and her family. He grew up in a house, and his family very honestly referred to his childhood home as a *house*. He rebutted with this very argument to his wife as she walked him to his car—that he had grown up in a house and could not fully accept why on earth a family (and most particularly his wife) would try so hard to live two realities at once. "You have to admit that it's not really a shack but a house, and it seems to me that you guys are trying to play a game with yourselves and others regarding the truth. Why do you and your brothers and your parents, when they were living, so badly need this to be a shack and not a home?"

She answered him this way (her head was poking inside the drivers' side window, and she was wearing nothing but a thin, gauzy nightgown that was being pock-marked with early morning drops of rain): "I do not know."

Naturally, when he drove to work after such an answer, he felt fatigued, but he also felt a kind of strange excitement too. When she had trotted away from the car after giving him her unsatisfying answer of *I do not know*, the rain had managed to make visible the line down the center of her buttocks.

As he drove into town, he found himself ruminating on the image of his wife jogging quickly back to a front door. At first, he felt a pleasurable pang as his memory slid down his wife's bottom, but then his mind focused on the front door. The door was intentionally made to look as though it were leaning and falling at the same time. The door jamb had been reclaimed from a carcass of an old dairy building where they made butter. When one first came upon the shack, there was a sense that the house had collapsed along with the bygone era of women with forearms and braided, fine, long hair for Sunday. It was only a sense though, and it was a deceiving one at that. There was no collapse, no carcasses—everything had been built new and intentionally to appear as though restless human abandonment and enduring reclaiming nature had left the goods for a crudely fashioned lean-to. The house was created to look as if a long dead manner of living had been found by a wandering desperate family, perhaps post-apocalypse, and turned into a clownish shanty castle with rust falls and steel roof waves and veins of greenery and chimney stones. The pang below his waist quickly became a wince in his neck as he saw the house in his mind.

The more he thought of the house, the angrier he became. He had not wanted to live in the house after his wife's mother had passed on. They had fought for some time over the issue. The house was a museum of his wife's family's genius and religious sense of art and intellect which somehow made the shack's pretense all the more annoying. Precious paintings lined the walls; often scholars made a trek to the house to study its contents. Letters of writers and poets and philosophers filled the drawers of rare, old desks and dressers. Precious sculptures and vases sat in kingly modesty on cluttered end tables and shaggy window sills. Once when he was courting his wife, a family cat had knocked over a rare Picasso ceramic sculpture, and all the family did was laugh. They left the sculpture where it fell and shattered. Later when his wife's father died, one of his father-in-law's friends made a little, polished headstone for the sculpture and set it down by the dusty remains.

There was something so clearly wrong with a counterfeit shack, and that was what tore into him; that was what he hated. He argued with his wife and her family in his mind as he drove from work back to the shack. The half hour drive was a courtroom. His workday always disappeared when he turned onto the mansion dotted country road that led to the shack. Indeed, he disappeared a little too. His life, his character, his world always evaporated as soon as he turned onto the shack's street. His work as an assistant district attorney did not count in their eyes. When he was in his world, his work counted a great deal as the victims' and the parents' of victims *thank you* cards covered his office walls. His chest genuinely, painfully tightened as he remembered his wife's friends wandering away from him when he told them what he did for a living. As he neared the shack, he even found himself wishing just a little that something very bad might happen to one of them, and then they very well might see the value in what he did; they could finally see what it felt like to actually be vulnerable (to actually be a victim). And for just a fleeting moment, as he pulled into the long, unpaved driveway of the shack, an image of his wife's best friend naked and beaten and violated and strangled came to his mind. His groin ached madly as it had unintentionally aroused him greatly.

He heard laughter when he got out of his car and walked with a sigh as he eyed the strange car in the driveway. The summer evening was honey bright. The house sat in deep, lush trees and bush, but a fine, clear path of handmade tile and brick lead one safely to the front *opening* (not *door* as shacks had openings and houses had doors) (he could never get a single member of his wife's family to call it a *door*). There was another tile and brick pathway that led to the backyard which was an expanse of lawn, gardens, and various improvised seating arrangements.

He followed the path that led to the backyard. He was the first to stop moving. When he had rounded the shack, he saw his wife and an unknown young man running around the lawn naked. The young man was chasing her, and she was laughing greatly at this and was running in darted directions with one arm wrapped around her torso as if the hilarity of the moment was so great that her insides just might burst out. The young man was the second one to stop moving. Finally, his wife. All three then stood very still with their arms hanging straight down at their sides.

The Lump
(Susanna)

When he first saw her, he didn't see her at all. It appeared to him as a lump. Simply a lump on the ground. Dark with a bit of pattern. Perhaps a pattern one would find on an oriental carpet or perhaps a hotel lobby curtain.

But the lump rose up and revealed a face the color of the moon.

He jumped back. He was expecting a lump, not a mix of silver and white and dark very dark brown eyes that were dark eyes that meant always to be dark—not some special occasion dark—no. These were born to look burnt. He asked her if she was okay, because rising lumps to this gentleman meant that certainly, things were not okay. He was hiking. He was standing erect, and his forearms had plump veins, and his skin was the color of a roasted chicken. He was just fine. But this lump. This lump with a moon colored face and two eyes that looked completely charred...well, you asked these sorts of finds if they are okay.

Well...as reasonable as his question was, it pissed her off, and the rising no longer lump told the just fine roasted man to fuck off.

Jesus, I just wanted to know if you were okay. But even as he said this his voice faded, for he realized her *fuck off* was more like a ripple from some other thrown pebble and not his presence.

"Help," she said with a parched, onion skin voice.

"Can you stand?" he asked.

She did not stand. Instead, she rolled onto her side. He was both relieved and horrified. It seemed his mountain senses were not wrong—she was, in fact, rolled in a carpet. She was completely naked underneath. As she turned, the stiff carpet buckled and could not cover a healthy strip of moon-colored breast. The man's eyes, though, did not stay on the surprise of bare breast but rather froze on a torn up foot.

"Your foot," he said in a kind of weak boom.

"My foot?" she asked, though it was clear it was not really a question rather a hollow echo.

Then the man felt an overwhelming urge to faint. It became quite clear that this carpet was hiding a great deal more than a bare bottom.

The girl then fainted for him.

He knelt down and scooped her up in his arms.

The heavy carpet made it nearly impossible for him to carry her steadily, but he could not remove it. He could not take away any more of this girl's dignity.

As he stumbled through the woods, his body began to burn and sweat from the old wool carpet. The crook in both his arms began to bleed from the intense friction. The sun was teasing away its light, and she was not waking up. *Oh don't die on me*, he moaned. Her head and one-and-a-half feet bobbed as he muscled his way *towards*. He was still quite far from his truck. He had no intention of returning to his truck in one day. He had intended on camping and thinking and maybe even catching his very own dinner.

The sun, completely on time, completely without a care, hugged only the silhouette of the trees. The sun now only wanted (but the sun just does just is) to blue up an otherwise colorless sky. The man began—out of both darkness and fatigue—to stumble. He had not fully fallen yet, but he could sense eminence. He kept on feeling what it would feel like to fall. He was so sincerely tired. He had gone to the woods to rest. To rest because he was so worn out. Now, his body burned in a way he never imagined it could, and his heart pounding with exercise, fear, and intense sympathy felt as though it would surely fail if he did not pause.

It was wholly dark when he draped her softly on the ground. He didn't know what to do. He was very thirsty, so his dry mouth told him to find water. He pulled a drought of water from the loud, black river that had talked to him the whole time he lumbered. Normally, rivers yell or moan or bubble and always they spoke in River, but this time this river talked and took the time to speak in *panic.*

Then, as if reason arose or as if fear had finally leveled off, the man tore off his shirt and began to bind her bleeding foot tightly. (He had intended on being at a hospital by now, but bringing limp, carpeted girls down mountains was not quite as easy as he thought.) He pushed open the carpet and saw to his small horror and bigger relief that while she had been heavily scraped and beaten, nothing more appeared to be *torn apart.* Because the foot was the worst he had ever seen. He stiffened like a boy-child as he rummaged through his backpack looking for something to put on her. He was almost frowning with purpose. His lips were tightly pursed, and his nostrils flared. His brain was flooding with the juice of *must do.*

He managed to put the girl in a flannel shirt and a pair of cotton boxers. The boxers were printed with playing cards, and it made him hate his ex-girlfriend even more. She had bought them for him and laughed when he opened the box on Christmas morning, and she had laughed when he first donned them. Now, seeing them on this girl only made the other girl—the one who laughed—seem so ugly it made the man shudder.

The man took one last deep breath and stood. That foot had to go to the hospital and this girl, even after water was dribbled onto her face and lips, was not waking up. He pulled out his flashlight and swung the girl over his shoulder, so he could maneuver the flashlight and distribute the girl's weight better. Never did he feel a deeper connection to a woman than he did the moment he wrapped his arm around her legs and buttocks. It was as if this was the first time a woman was still enough to not flicker—still enough to actually be felt.

The dark woods crunched with complete mystery underneath his possessed boots. After an hour of plunging, the pain of numerous stumbles and scrapes faded, and the awkward weight of an unconscious woman fell into a rhythm. The flashlight was now barely necessary. The flashlight spotted countless trees, occasional animals, and pine needle carpeted ground.

"What is your name?" he would ask out loud.

"Almost fell there," he would say. He would then have this crazy sense of pride for not dropping her as he thundered down the black mountain that was not meant to be tackled in one day.

"I am so going to have a beer when I get down from this goddamn mountain," he would say. "She suggested that I go. She suggested that I get over her and that this mountain was going to be good for me," he said to the woman draped over his shoulder. Then he whispered, and this whisper was the saddest thing he ever bothered the unconscious girl with, "The truth is I never was into her...and that was what messed me up."

When the heavy steel forester gate jumped into

the hazy circle of flashlight light, the man broke into a run. He could smell the dawn (which smells a little more hopeful than *wet*) as he drew a line between his eyes and his ancient Bronco. It was brown and white with bumper stickers instead of body work.

He draped her gently in the back seat and then paused. He did not want her so far from him. He scooped her up and draped her in the front seat. He then drove them with a speed that made his old beast vibrate.

The town's hospital was small, but strangely (at least it was strange enough for his mind to think of it) well-appointed and modern. Nurses and an Indian doctor buzzed and yelled around them. Another female doctor pounced on them and pulled him and started to bark out questions.

I found her near the top of the mountain. No, she was conscious. She passed out and has been out. I'm okay. Stitches? Just a glass of water. Is she okay? Can I sit down for a moment?

The girl, the lump, after almost frantic shouting from the staff, was wheeled away. He did not like her away. But sitting and water and clear, bright florescent light felt intensely good, so he was able to tune out a little and just sit in the emergency's inner sitting bay.

"How is she?" he asked a grave nurse.

"The police are here. She's in surgery. The foot and they will have to see what else," answered the nurse.

Near the top of the mountain. Yes, I can take

you there. She was. No, I didn't see anyone else on the mountain. I followed the river down. There was. A carpet. I had to leave it. Yes, I can take you to it. She was rolled in it. At first yes, but then she passed out. No, didn't say anything...except fuck off...and help. Fuck off. Yes, but she was pretty already gone. No, I didn't look around. I just grabbed her and ran her down the mountain. For just a second to bind her foot. Her foot was torn up. And to get her out of the carpet. No. I had to put her in my shirt and some box...ers. Pretty beaten. Scrapes. I didn't though, look too close. I.

"Is he well enough? Nurse?" asked the cop. (The man looked worse than he felt.)

"I can take you now," said the man.

"They may be still up there," said the cop.

"They?" asked the man.

"Someone had to have done this," returned the cop.

"Do you know who she is?" asked the man.

"We think so. We found an abandoned car around ten miles from the base of the mountain with a flat tire and an open purse on the passenger-side seat. Hang on...." The cop then held up his cell phone. The police officer put away his phone and hung his head. "They've got her husband here," said the officer with a wet, intense choke.

The man rose to his feet as if someone had grabbed him by his shirt and pulled him up. Never had it occurred to him that she would have a husband, and now that she did, he was feeling something, but it was so big and choking and terrifyingly neutral that all the man wanted to do is get back to the business of helping the police. Get back up that mountain. She had a husband; he, her husband, would have to deal with the business of her being a nearly dead lump.

It was not lost on the man as he climbed the mountain that once again he was climbing a mountain for a woman. Or rather, because of a woman. Or even better, he was interacting with a woman, and now he had to climb a mountain. The morning sky was a matte gray. Climbing underneath it with a half dozen police and a half dozen forest rangers felt better than when he was climbing it alone in the sun just the day before. This preference disturbed the climbing, now thoroughly exhausted man. The worse thought that floated through his mind was, “Finally a woman that has pulled me into life. This is so much life. I have never lived this much life. Finally, not just waking up and working and taking the train.”

The carpet was found. Then the man and the officers rose higher to where the lump was first roused. Then they circled the area and found an iron stake hammered into the ground. It was neatly (and with much grave calm) ascertained that the woman’s foot was impaled at that spot. They must have staked her to the ground right there. As the man and the police officer he had met at the hospital looked at the bloodied stake, a forest ranger was vomiting a little way off. The worse thing that floated through the man's mind was, "Wow. This is so intense, and I can handle it all. I was never sure if I could handle something like this and I can. I'm not throwing up."

Husbands are curious animals, and the man would realize this when he came down off the mountain and returned to the hospital. He was now almost tacitly attached to the older, non-vomiting police officer. The older officer mumbled to the man as they walked down the hospital corridor that this was the worst part, "I have been at this for a long time but husbands...telling husbands...Jesus."

This husband was cored and more scared than the man had ever seen another man. The husband's voice was soft and reserved. He ran his worked hands through his thinning hair, and he took off his square glasses and rubbed the ridge of his nose. He hung onto one elbow then dropped his arms and rocked. A doctor whisked him away before the husband could completely fall to the ground and beg God to take him and then beg God to let him take someone with him. Husbands want their wives to live, but just as badly they want their wives' attackers to die. The old police officer knew this and could see the murder ahead. There was no stopping them. Husbands.

"I want to see her," thought the man. "This is her husband," thought the man, "I want to see her alive. Damn. A husband. I never thought that she would have a husband," thought the man.

All the way home, he thought of the girl and daydreamed and wondered what she was like, or would be like with him, and then he would experiment with what she was like with her husband. Many times, he visualized what must have happened to her on the mountain. However, these were only seen in dream form. He only dreamt about her attack—never did he daydream about it. He only daydreamed about what she was like with her husband and then what she would be like with him. Sadly, or compassionately, the man never remembered his dreams. So, often he felt odd and removed, because his brain did not allow for him to process what happened—*really* happened on that mountain and the stake and the lump with a torn-up foot and how it all happened. However, his mind, above and out of reach, did think of the mountain and the total horror of it. His extra drinking and him constantly missing his train stop were the signs that his mind was dealing with the trauma. But his perfect work performance and charming first, second, and even third date with a charming special education teacher revealed that his brain would not let his conscious mind know the shocking truth.

When the phone call came, the man was not able to answer. This was a lucky occurrence, because it allowed the man to play the message of her voice over and over.

"Um. Oh boy, this is weird. My name is Susanna Gunther. I'm the girl you saved. You found on Mount Jay. The mountain you carried (long pause) I want to meet you. I guess again, well you know, awake. I have a gift for you...and well, I think (longish pause) I'm real bad with leaving messages (very brief nervous laughter)." This was played over and over.

Her house, or worse, *their house*, was set back in the woods. Enough land was cleared for a humble blue colored house with a cinderblock chimney and rusty oil drums filled with cleared woods. The walkway to the front door was a curious expression of optimism. It had (it was) a fresh, winding brick walkway that led to a semi-hammered-out cement stoop. The man assumed that it too would become brick. Someday. And that was the best way to describe the house and the land. Someday. But the house also showed that things happen (very bad things). So, some houses and some clearings are left for someday.

He could smell his impending dinner before he knocked on the splintered wooden door that might have been painted red. It smelled like something he might have had as a child. A subtle burn of fat and smoke of bake. A hover of sour that ran into butter and onion. The man had no saliva in his mouth, and the idea of having to sit at some unknown table with some unknown family and eat a mélange of all that this earth offered seemed like yet another impossibility in his life he was going to do anyway. He knocked on the door and found a surprised smile almost brutally pulled from his numb face.

Two wildly giggling children swung the door open and laughed and screamed, "Momma the good man is here. Momma! Hi!" The children did not come close to him but wanted to, so they piled over and over each other. It was a knot of blushing, freckled children.

The man could not help but chuckle. And he did. The good man.

But then she came and the man almost, but never did he or ever would he, cried. He did shut his eyes. It was not a blink but a full closure. She reached out and touched his wrist. "Come in," she said softly, "Kids let the man through," she said with forced humor. The man opened his eyes and touched his wrist where she had touched it.

She looked down, and before another expression or word or interaction could happen, the husband appeared and shook his hand with not much like in his eyes and said *come on in*.

The men had a beer, and the woman set the table. They covered professions. Both men felt ambiguous about their work, so they were able to take each other in in big gulps. The husband was taller and older. The man was more handsome and less responsible. She joined them for their third beer. She drank a generic orange soda and kept on letting her children have generous sips from it. Her clothes were old and out of fashion. The man figured they were her same clothes from high school and the effect was both sad and erotic. She was slim. Slight with narrow hips. But he knew all that. She wore no makeup, and her skin was the color of white sand. She had brown eyes that appeared freakishly big behind her thick, plastic framed glasses. Her hair was cottony with a river-like wave. It was very dark brown like her eyes.

The husband should have been grateful, but he could only feel hatred and shame in the presence of the man.

The man wanted desperately to have a moment alone with her, but there was so much pot roast and children and sulking husband. He knew by the time the homemade pie was served that this would be it. He had hoped—prayed even—that a friendship could be forged. His plan was to become friends with both, so he could see her throughout. But by the time he bit into his last bite of pie, he looked up and saw it all. He looked up and saw the husband staring at him with two huge plates of water over his eyes and not a bite of pie taken.

"I better go," said the man after he *saw it all.*

"But coffee," she said.

"The man said he has to go," the husband said. He was evaporating. The husband was turning into steam which is a really bad thing in the woods; anywhere else it is not good, but in the woods, it is really bad.

The man stood up and walked to the door in such a way that he felt afraid just by the way he was finding himself walking. Only a couple times, late night, in the city, had the man walked that way. The whole friendship plan with both Susanna and her husband made the man feel more embarrassed than ever.

Once again, he found himself drawing a line

with his eyes between him and his old Bronco, and once again, his life was weird because of this odd woman that he at first thought was a lump.

He climbed in with a sigh.

"Wait!" she yelled.

The man wanted to slam his head on the steering wheel.

She was carrying something. "Don't mind him," she said, "Please, let me thank you. I have a gift for you. My husband doesn't know how to handle all this."

"Do you?" hit back the man. Then the man felt horrible. Her children were standing on the jack-hammered porch and staring at their mother as if she were the whole world.

The woman nervously looked at the man then looked over her shoulder. The children caught their momma's eye and yelled, "Momma! Momma! Look!"

Painfully the woman addressed her children, "Yes?"

"Look!" they demanded.

"What?" asked the woman with a touch of anguish in her voice.

"The moon!" they yelled, "What color is the moon, Momma?"

One of her tiny wrists was draped over the driver's side window ledge of the man's Bronco, and this wrist was trembling. "Baby the moon?" she shot back with not a lot of voice.

"What color is it!" they demanded in a desperate attempt to get their momma back to their world.

"Baby, it's silver and white mixed," sighed the woman.

"Here," she said to the man, "I made this for you. And know that you will always. Always just know. Just know."

"Momma!" they yelled.

"I'm coming," returned the woman. The woman dropped the pile on top of the man's lap and returned to her little someday home.

The whole way home not once did he touch it, barring his lap that had no choice. He knew, because he had to check his speed, that it was a quilt.

His home was dark. He lived on the first floor of a big, old house. He entered and turned on one light. He opened up the quilt and saw his flannel shirt and his playing-card boxers transformed into a pattern of utter sadness, purity, earth, beauty, innocence, the woman, her romance, tenderness, life. He moved to the center of his house wrapped his body tightly with the quilt and sunk to the floor.

fuck off

fuck off

fuck off

"Fuck off," he whispered. In a dropping, chanted line.

And of all the things that the man finally found connection to, that the man attached to, understood of his sense of woman and love and connection was her telling him up on that mountain to

carry me down.

The Leitmotif Was a Felid (Catherine)

Cat sat at the bar in the position to become Bad Cat. Time and events had spun a little too quickly (even for a cat), and now she found herself dressed and drinking solely to have decisions made for her like seeds in the wind. Her tight, strapless dress pushed her bosom up into two perfect expressions of care, silk, and smother. Dozens of thick gold chains, anchored with diamond charms, hung from her tender neck. Her neck was barely visible. The armor was a curious contradiction to her almost painful bareness. Her skin was the exact color of a sugar cookie and was completely blank excepting for a handful of moles. Cat was never sure exactly how the gold chain giving started, but now that it had, she feared that if the gold chains were removed, her neck, like the Padaung Karen women of Burma, would collapse. Sometimes in drunker, more lighthearted moments, Cat would doodle pictures of her head flopping off and rolling into a swimming pool.

* * *

The light was so blinding that Cat was sure she would die, or that she, in fact, was dead. In Cat's first struggle to get up, she saw a pile of gold on a white metal cart. The pile looked wretchedly powerless under the green fluorescent light. Cat then clawed at her neck and began to scream. "Somebody, hold this girl down," shouted a man wearing an aquamarine frock and mask. A heavy woman wearing a flowered apron-like shirt ran to Cat, pricked her in the arm, and the lights went out for Cat.

* * *

"You are so completely lovely, Cat," said Dr. Stratton. "How can it be that you can be so completely lovely?" said the man as they stood in the entryway, taking off their raincoats. It was clear he was very proud of what he had arrived with.

Cat eyed her date, the young doctor, before her. He was just almost handsome, and just almost wealthy. She had gone to this party with Dr. Stratton against her better judgment. It was a young doctors' party. Stratton had invited her, but she barely knew him. They had met at a bar. When he called her a few days later to invite her to the party, she spent most of the time during their longish telephone conversation wondering who he was, and *had they really talked so much at the Red Room*, as he appeared to have known a great deal about her. Dr. Stratton was a young doctor, and Cat never liked young or doctor. There was so much arrogance that still hadn't truly been bought yet. The brand-new leather furniture, brand new British stereo system, and brand new, pretty dates all collided with the small apartment with laminated kitchen cupboards and framed posters passing as art. To Cat, this showed everything. Nothing displeased her more than the folly of grabbing for the big things before teasing out the finer details.

"So Stratton, who's your lovely friend?" asked the male host of the party whose eyes were clearly stroking Cat.

Cat recoiled.

* * *

"Cat!" begged the man soaking in the rain. "Cat! Please be reasonable."

Cat stood in the rain in front of a swing-set in the middle of a Wednesday night. The man was a boy. He was Cat's age. Twenty-one. Cat had known him in high school which always made Cat uneasy, because she always forgot she had ever gone. He wore corduroys and pullover windbreakers. His hair was soft, thick gold, and his skin still puckered.

Cat had run into him at a Korean barbecue take-out place. He stared at her dumbly for a full minute before he could ask her how she had been. She had been better, and they spent the night smoking pot in his dorm room and having sex until all four feet were cramped. He would keep little treats for her in his pocket. Sometimes it would be a little tin of hard toffees; sometimes it would be a photocopy of a funny cartoon; sometimes it would be a live pumping heart. He was like that. He kept his love in his windbreaker pocket for her to reach in and take it, or if she wouldn't reach in and take it, he would put his shaking hand inside his pocket and pull it out for her.

* * *

"Jesus, Cat," softly said the Man. The Man was holding a bouquet of roses and was uneasily striding towards Cat's hospital bed. The Man was wearing gray slacks, a plaid button-down shirt, and a black leather coat. The Man was in his fifties. Cat had been his mistress. Cat lived in the condo that he had purchased for them. Cat could no longer bear his presence, and he gently let her escape. He signed the condo solely over to Cat. He just couldn't handle the idea of Cat not living under the roof he had bought for them.

Tears flooded the Man's sloped, brown eyes. He reached out to brush a lock of hair off Cat's thick fringe of eyelashes.

Cat brushed his hand and her hair away. "How did you know I was here?" asked Cat bitterly. She knew how he knew. She just wanted him to tell her.

"Cat," moaned the Man, "If he weren't following you, you would have died."

"*He* wasn't following me...you were...you had been since the end...since the beginning," returned Cat in a voice that would have preferred to have been the voice of a porch swing or a door hinge.

With a shaky hand, the Man held out a heavy gold chain with a marble-sized diamond swinging innocently, like a star children envision for wishing, over Cat's bosom.

Cat snatched it sharply.

* * *

The Red Room was a vast place that was filled with travelers. Choosing a hotel's bar, opulent with wood paneling and a ceiling mural, made Cat feel all the more resolved to get lost. The bartender looked far too young for his coatless tuxedo and clientele. Cat hated ordering from him. His eyes shivered down her spine. For a moment, Cat envisioned her spine curling out of her skin and lashing up at the bartender. Her sharp, rattling bones, menacingly clicking would snag and bite his puffy cheek and then recoil back into her body. The only hitch to Cat's spine fantasy was that Cat could not decide if her spine would strike quickly, like a scorpion's tail or languidly like a Lion's mood.

"Can I buy you a drink?" asked a tall, heavily developed man beside her.

"Cat," she answered.

The man smiled curiously and ordered two drinks. "My name is Stratton...Dr. Stratton...what is your name?" he asked while sipping heavily off his beer.

Cat eyed him. Had she not been asked that, and had she not answered? And for a moment Cat's heart jumped. Her first night—of breaking away from the boy—and already one of his threats seemed to be coming true. *Cat, never again will you find anyone who will understand you the way I do.*

* * *

The doctor and Cat were walking up to her condominium, and the boy was curled in the bushes. Or was he not? Was he just standing there? The weather kept on shifting between fog and rain that night, and so did the position of the boy. Cat kissed the doctor and sent the boy away. No, Cat kissed the doctor and sent the doctor away. The boy yelled at the doctor, and the doctor insisted he stay with Cat. Cat held onto her earlier resolve to send the doctor away.

"Cat we need to talk," drooled the boy.

Cat stood with keys in hand. Keys that opened up to a fortress.

"Cat, please," he cried.

"Let's walk," sternly and quietly answered Cat.

Cat shoved her hands in her pockets as she shoved her high heels into the wet sidewalk. The wind was blowing water, as if it were sand, against Cat's face. The shifting moody weather led them to a park that was just a few blocks from Cat's home. Cat and the boy had been there often. They stopped at the swing set where the boy promptly reminded Cat that it was this very spot that Cat had told him that she loved him.

"No, I didn't," rebuffed Cat.

The boy began to tremble.

"You said that you loved me, but I did not answer. That is what happened *at this very spot,*" snapped Cat.

"No, Cat, no," mumbled the boy. The boy's face shifted...like the night. Rain began to spill and pour as if the clouds had slipped and lost their contents and composure. A tender, broken expression of optimism quivered over the boy's face. "Cat...Cat I have something for you...." The boy patted his right pocket. "And something in this one too...." The boy then patted his left pocket.

Cat inhaled and then angrily exhaled. "Stop it," she groaned. "Just stop it," she whispered.

The boy first mouthed his words then cried them out as if they were meant more for him than her. "Cat!" begged the boy. "Cat! Please be reasonable."

Cat made an early gesture of walking away. The boy grabbed her arm.

"Just let me give you my gifts...just let me do that...it's all I ask...you can then walk away...leave me forever."

Cat dropped her shoulders and her turning stance. "Okay," she sighed.

The boy reached into his pocket, and the clouds stood up embarrassed and spilled out. The streetlights almost seemed to be blinking—from utter disbelief—into the now rainless, shockingly wet landscape. Cat leaned on one foot. The boy slightly stuck out his tongue as he pulled out the thick gold chain.

"For you," be beamed.

Cat was not paying attention.

"For you," he repeated only this time Cat was paying attention. He sensed this and deftly, intuitively, tightened his grip and caught her rising arm.

Gulp was all Cat could do.

"Want me to put it on for you? Or do you want to admire it a little more?" The boy was dangling the skinned kitten just breaths away from Cat's howling eyes. (Her mouth could not howl; all the cotton in a spring sky was now crammed into her throat and mouth.) The gold chain was wound around the kitten's neck. It looked just like a collar. The boy's grip tightened. Cat and the boy were sure he was going to break her arm. "Now, Cat, are you ready for gift number two?" taunted the boy with a grimy slur. The boy then pulled Cat deep within his torso. "And then you can leave me forever," he whispered into her quaking ear. The boy pushed a knife into her stomach.

* * *

The bar she was drinking at was different than any bar she had ever visited. It had been a month since her *event*. It was a curious bar indeed. Everything, including the patrons, was, at first glance, in black and white, but with a few seconds of contemplation, they became ordinary. The drinks were flavorless until she decided how they should taste. Even the music was only present if she wanted music present, and Cat loved watching all the patrons bob or not bob their heads according to her preference. The effect of the bar was seeping deeply within her.

Her Dr. Stratton was, no doubt, somewhere saving lives (yet nothing mattered less to her). Cat could always tell when she was about to turn bad, when it was clear that the current chain-giver was doomed. She wondered if anyone in the room would touch her bare upper back that evening. She wondered if this time there would be many leading up to her doctor's sack or just one talented thief? She thought all of this in a kind of lazy, languid way as it did not matter how it happened. It never did.

* * *

"Here you go, Cat," playfully smirked Dr. Stratton as she was having her belly checked by another doctor.

"What?" asked Cat. Cat was annoyed that

somehow Dr. Stratton knowing her attending physician meant he could come along to all her check-ups.

Dr. Stratton knew the doctor that had stitched Cat back together and had used this association to continue knowing where Cat was. Cat eventually accepted this and moved from her condo to Dr. Stratton's apartment.

"How am I?" asked Cat.

The physician smiled widely and told her that she was now perfectly healthy and perfectly fine and perfectly (*he might add*) beautiful.

Cat smiled weakly and slanted her eyes towards Dr. Stratton who was dangling a long gold chain with a bejeweled mouse swimming beneath it.

"A mouse...Cat...isn't that great?" he beamed.

The Grasshopper
(Della)

The grasshopper was not green like the ones Della had imagined in her mind, or, at least, the grasshopper Della held was not like the ones she had remembered. The grasshopper was sandy-colored with spots and swipes of dark, not black, not brown. Nature's dark. The grasshopper's body was tidy and compact. Its legs, while extended backward and slim, seemed more strong than delicate. There was no sense of fragility or looseness in the creature.

John, her husband, had asked her if she wanted to hold the grasshopper. He was bent over, smiling. His feet were invisible in the thick, park grass. Nervously Della agreed, and her mind then instantly flashed to another splice with nature. It had been truly a defeat. She and her husband were driving through a neighboring town when suddenly he swerved over to the side of the road.

"Oh no," he said as he hopped out of the car.

Della, pulled by habit, followed him to the curb. He was stooped over next to a public mailbox. His brown, wavy hair touched the chipped, blue metal.

"It needs a place to dry out," he said as he lifted a large lavender butterfly up from a patch of rain-soaked cement.

Carefully, with cupped hands, John slid into the car. Della assisted with the particulars; it felt like taking grandmother to church; she shut his door carefully, making sure the seat belt and the hem of his coat were safely tucked inside the car.

"Hold him while I drive...I need to find a place for him to dry out," he said.

John handed Della the butterfly. The butterfly panicked and wildly fanned her hands. The sensation was frightening and terrible. "I can't handle this," she said as her husband searched for a safe place for butterflies to dry out.

Della's husband drove in an exaggerated position. His head was almost above the steering wheel, and his elbows were tightly pressed against his sides. "Hang on...I see a little creek," he said.

Almost angrily and very unexpectedly, Della tossed the butterfly out of her cupped hands. It tumbled away—without flight—and disappeared between the seats.

Her husband pulled up to the creek. An out-of-place row of small houses sat across the street from the creek. They were all sided with stucco and painted in pastel colors. The houses were decayed and fallen, and Della had hoped at first sight they were abandoned, because they seemed so completely unfit as homes, but almost-fresh toys and garbage were scattered in front of the houses. The derelict row of homes made her sad.

John, with his body and legs half out of the car, searched sadly for the rejected butterfly. It was still alive. "Come here, guy," said Della's husband tenderly as he teased the tissue-like creature out of the vinyl ravine.

Della stood next to the car—both of the car doors were left wide open—feeling too ashamed to witness the happy ending as her husband walked towards a sparse stand of trees and tall weeds next to the creek.

Nervously Della agreed. She was expecting an uncomfortable tickle when John placed the grasshopper in her quick-cupping hands. Instead, she only felt soft weight: a life that weighed as much as a candle's flame. A smile flew up in her face. Della lifted her right hand. The grasshopper, who toured better than a gentleman (*I am a grasshopper. What joy! What luck!*), paused as if to indulge her with a clear view of a real grasshopper: the absolute whole nature of the grasshopper. Then, with the most extravagant mix of lightness, strength, and direction, the grasshopper sprung into the air—he appeared gilded in the still-thick, late afternoon sun—and landed ten feet away from her in the rough, green grass.

Bitches

The Developer
(Carrie Ann)

He was flying to Asia on his way to wrap up one of the largest deals of his career, and all he could do was think that he was this wealthy, successful, forty-seven-year-old male who could only think in terms of the past, and he had to do something, because kings must fight, and he knew that being tethered by the past keeps one from picking fights. And he desperately wanted the mood for blood on his sword.

Quite plainly, it began in the grocery store. It was an ordinary grocery store in a small town in Central New York. It was very hot out. Clothes were sticking to everybody. Our man was in a suit. A fact that should have told him more about his character, his needs, and his world. However, at the time, he was so hot and was so tired of driving that when he entered the grocery store, he had completely forgotten that he was wearing a very fine navy suit.

He needed to buy things to eat. He had rented a small cottage by Seneca Lake, and he was hungry and hot and tired of driving. He needed food. The cottage he had rented would not be stocked with any food or drink. The grocery store was huge and bright and cool. But it was hot enough outside that everyone's clothes—even inside the air-conditioned store—were still sticking to their bodies.

As our gentleman stood in line with a handbasket filled with bananas, sliced ham, tomatoes, crackers, salami, cheddar cheese, toilet paper, paper towels, aspirin, batteries, cereal, milk, and a magazine about this awful world of ours, he profoundly regretted his choice of handbasket. If he had thought to get a cart, he would have bought potatoes, charcoal, lighter fluid, steaks, and a little barbecue of which they had several to choose from. He would have bought maybe some berry ice-cream and maybe some vegetables. He might have even bought some sunscreen and a pair of rubber flip-flops. Even stuff to make chili would have been considered if he had taken the cart. However, he never does. He never takes a cart. He always thinks that he is a single male, and all he really needs is just a basket.

She did not mean to grab his hand. She did not, and he knew that, but still, her grabbing his hand (over bananas no less) sent off this sort of primal want. It's like *you grabbed me...now I want to grab you*. The man was not completely sure how all of this grab stuff worked with the human animal, but he knew that when he gets grabbed, he looks up at the grabbee and thinks *now I want to grab you.* Generally, if our man (after being grabbed or somehow poked, touched, bumped, etc...) looks up and it's a man or an ugly girl, he thinks *you asshole or you bitch*—something like that. However, this grabber (who reached for the bananas as he was placing them on the conveyor belt) was cute. And her pants were sticking to her ass. She looked to be around twenty. She was not. He found out at the little cottage he was renting that she was seventeen. As she rung up his groceries, she would turn around and put his stuff in a paper bag. Her butt was round, a little big for his normal taste; however, our gentleman was under the whole primal grab-me grab-you thing. She was wearing thin, white cotton pants. He hated them. They looked just like nurse pants. She had on white underwear, and he kept on running his eyes over the thicker, whiter rims of the things. He felt they had to have been cotton and purchased in a plastic bagged multi-pack that he often saw in drugstores. And while they were completely horrible to him, they did appear to be literally holding her butt which caused a sort of surprising feeling of anxiousness, maybe even a little jealousy.

He had the cash, but he used his credit card so she would know his name. Her long, blonde, curly, horrid (to him)—maybe dyed, maybe permed—hair touched the face of his card when she turned it over and studied his signature. However, there was something to this girl. Our man, still pretty bitter, always remembers their first encounter with a bit of harshness regarding her appearance and overall comportment, but even with criticisms, he never allowed his memory to forget or fog the fact that when he saw her handling his credit card, he found himself getting aroused. And our gentleman did do some soul searching when he looked back at their first encounter as how his credit card could have been so completely woven into his person—for as she handled his card, he found himself with a semi-soft boner in the check-out line. When she handed him back his card, he grabbed her hand and gently squeezed her fingers. They were very soft and fine boned, and it almost felt like sex squeezing them. He looked into her bespeckled eyes as he squeezed her fingers, and it was clear to him that she had the look of utter surprise and fear. Right then and there, he knew why he only grabbed the handbasket. He was going to have to return to this grocery store daily, because handbaskets can only carry so much, and every time he was going to use his credit card and grope her hand. *And*, he thought to himself, *she would soon look for me, fear me, and masturbate nightly about this older man who quite obviously wants her*. He could always see it—the scene of her pleasuring herself because of him. He always saw an *I Love Jesus* sign made out of knotty oak hanging just above her bed (now this was not *really* true, for he never did go to her home) (however, this was what he thought would most likely be true). She would be wearing some little tank top or amusement park t-shirt and those big, fucking, white cotton panties, and she would slip those lovely, fair fingers inside the sticky cotton, and she would think about him touching her, wanting her, wanting her, wanting her. *There was nothing more irresistible to a woman,* believed our man, *than to be wanted. Forget about gifts. Forget about love. Forget about looking good or acting nice for a woman. Just want, old boys. Just want them.*

After a few days of regular shopping, our man knew he had to make a more concrete move. He knew, because he kept on finding himself sitting on his deck overlooking Seneca Lake, drinking a beer, and thinking that she was going to appear. He would hear a dog bark or wheels on gravel and somehow think she was going to stop by his cottage. Somehow, she had figured out where the stranger—*the developer*—lived, and the mystery and sexiness of all his grocery shopping would have finally driven her to his door. Sometimes, he fantasized, she would skip the front door, walk around the cottage, and come up from behind as he was sitting in his deck chair. He would then grab her wrists and pull her tightly against the back of the chair. However, those were only wishes, phantoms. Each night on the lake for our man was quiet and alone. He also saw a change in him that he had not previously seen. Our man had just turned forty, and he noticed that while he most likely in his twenties and even thirties could have sustained himself on self-pleasuring with the grocery store girl, he found, however, at forty that he could barely even get the political will to touch himself, as he so badly, so completely, needed to get her for real. Somehow after turning forty, the dream was not enough to sustain him.

A few sentences back, in the previous paragraph, it was introduced—although not flat out—what our man did for a living. Our man was a developer. He traveled the world and bought land or got a group of investors to buy a property, and he would then build structures on the land that was purchased. He sometimes kept the development, or sometimes he would sell it and move on. He was in the Finger Lake region of New York, because he wanted to investigate all the dirt-cheap lakeside property. And never once did our man feel guilty as he simultaneously enjoyed the land's beauty and the potential it had for development. He was, after all, a developer. He was not an appreciator. It's also important to note, however, that he was not a robber. He only bought what was for sale. *If this town wants its land to remain pristine, then they should not sell it to me*, often thought the man as he peered out onto the lake. *No matter how beautiful something is, I will build on top of it, and I will either sell it or leave it and collect rent.*

It had been a shitty day for our man, our developer. *Meetings, fucking meetings, all day at city hall. I hate small town mayors. They are all fucking liars. If you currently live in a small town, from here on out make it a practice to actively hate your mayor.* The mayor was telling our man that the town will sell the lakeside land. Then the mayor would tell the local newspaper that he was not sure if he was going to sell it to the developer. Then the mayor would inform our man, our developer, that he could get matching state funds to develop (as long as there was ample public access). Then our man would call his contact at the state capitol only to find that nothing had been done. *Fucker*, our man would think as he drove to city hall from his lakeside cottage, *The council members were not much better than that fucking mayor—though at least they were not lying so much. They seemed more bored than anything. Some really did seem to hate me and everything I stood for, and if I ever found myself broken down on the side of the highway at the dead of night in the middle of a blizzard, they would (even though they love Jesus with all their hearts) just drive on.* Our man always laughed hysterically when he recalled one of the council members saying that to him at a particularly heated meeting. Not all of the city council was against our man. Some thought he could make some money for the town. All in all, it was a mixed crowd, and our man thought they smelled a little like tuna and oranges.

After an especially terrible day at city hall, our man knew he needed groceries. He screamed into the parking lot with a great deal of speed, because he could not punch the mayor in the face. Our gentleman did lighten up a bit when a very old lady flipped him off, because he almost hit her with his BMW. Our man laughed hysterically when it happened. He loved seeing such an old and proper lady flipping the bird. *Life can be too fucking fabulous when you least expect it*, he thought to himself as he got out of his car and headed towards the grocery store entrance.

When he got inside, he felt a kind of funny exhilaration that only arrives when you have had a completely shitty day. A day can be so bad that a sort of recklessness or abandon arises. Our man, once again, filled his little handbasket with food and another magazine about how horrible this world is. In line, he grabbed her repeatedly with his eyes, and she then turned to him and said, *it's you again*. Our man then said, *yes*. He went on to say something like he did not how to eat or cook and that he wondered if she would come over to his little lakeside cottage and help him out. She laughed a little and wrote down her number. She then handed him a hot pink post-it note with her phone number on it. The sticky strip of the post-it note annoyed the crap out of our man, and now after some time has passed, he saw that as a clear sign, a clear omen: she had handed him something that was meant to be *stuck somewhere*—not *handed to*. He peeled her sticky post-it off the inside of his hand and slipped it in his wallet. He grimaced as it buckled and dragged against the bills. He then looked her in the eyes and said that he was going to call her as soon as he got home. She then said she would have to shower before she would *dooooo* anything. Mind you, that *do* was so accurate you can never know, but it's important for our man that you do know that this girl never said *do*. No, she said *dooooo*. And as our man now contemplates that do and when he first encountered that do of hers, he is amazed by how many signs there were that this was a bad deal. *Dooooo*, at first, he thought she was just stupid or maybe like the council members, bored or tired. Only later would he realize that that *dooooo* was emphatic. She was pressing him. *Jesus, all this fucking shit I never saw.*

So she came over. Our gentleman showered, knowing that after all, she was going to. Our man was like that. If someone says they are going to shower first., then he showers too. Like if someone says I've got a surprise for you, he comes up with a surprise too. He answered the door. He was a little taken aback by out of work grocery store girl. He was not prepared for the clown makeup or the gallons of perfume and the gum chewing and the slightly tacky, slightly slick heavy application of body lotion that smelled a little bit like a freshly cleaned toilet.

He took her to his amazing back deck. He put some good, age-neutral music on and hustled towards her with some good wine. Her raccoon eyes spotted the bottle a mile away, and before he could even tell her it was from California, she narrowed her eyes and asked if she could have some seven-up with that wine. Our gentleman laughed and suggested that, *why don't we include a shot of vodka in the mix and make it a good drink?* She then said, *good idea.* And so, our gentleman turned around and made a pitcher of wine, vodka, and while he did not have seven-up, he thought beer would do. They drank a few pitchers and argued outside on his fabulous lakefront deck. It appeared that he was (and while this was not a direct quote—it does nail most of the spirit, if not all of the words) *a dick.* In fact, he was called one so many times that as the special cocktails were hitting him, he just sort of answered to it like a pet name. She would say something like *Jesus, you are such a dick*, and he would then ask her if she would like some more mixed grill. And mind you, throughout all of this, that was just what our man was doing. Often our man thought of the imbalance of the sexes—especially regarding courtship and dating. *Women will just never understand that as they are arguing with us—calling us dicks—we are making special cocktails and grilling meats and asking you if you are cold and wanting to kiss you. And it's doubly important to note that while we are handling live fire, insults, and extreme horniness, we are really drunk. You ladies will just never understand.*

This little scene of eating, drinking, and arguing continued on the back deck for some time. Weeks could almost be used to describe what the scene felt like for our man. Sex was still looming. It was after a week or so when our man started to refer to his grocery store girl as his map girl. On nights she came over, she would let him run his fingers over a new state but never let him lay his body on the whole map of America. However, for our gentleman, our developer, it was okay. Work had been hard, so tender knees and pink puffy things that all seemed to taste the same on her was enough.

It was now the end of July, and it was time for our man to go. With Seneca Lake, he won a little and lost a little. He was allowed to put up a hotel, and they did get matching funds, but he had to shell out for some big park on the lake and had to make the hotel's dock public. The final night with map girl was okay too. She didn't call him a dick so much, and she let him cruise the mid-west (his favorite) but still no USA. And she actually made the special cocktails for them on their final night. This was a real favor, as he always got depressed dumping exceptional wine into a pitcher filled with beer and vodka. Our man knew he could have used cheap wine, but a man can only go so far to get laid, and cheap wine for him was too far.

Our man did drive by the grocery story on his way back to Massachusetts. He didn't stop in though. He was not hungry nor was he tired of driving, and somehow at that moment, he thought the only way he was ever going to go into that store and see that girl again was when he was hungry and tired of driving. The open highway felt great in his car. He loved his car. He truly did love his car. His car was his family. It was stunningly hot and bright out, and he had a six-hour drive ahead of him in which he could daydream about America...that ever elusive experience. Shortly after he passed Albany, he had to take a super piss. He had drunk about four diet cokes, and he was dying. He stopped at a thruway stop and bought all sorts of stupid crap. He had this ongoing flirt thing with one of the girls in his office, and he always brought her stupid crap from his many outings. One time, he even brought her back a loaf of bread.

He opened his trunk, jumped back, and yelped, because the brass Statue of Liberty fell on his flip-flopped foot, and all she said was *hi*. He then ordered her out of his trunk, but she remained. He then asked her why she was in his trunk, and before she could answer, he told her that he could not have girls in his trunk. And then she looked up at him, with her horribly over-painted eyes, and said, "But I've graduated from high school." Our man was so confused. How on earth does one go from *get out of my trunk* to *but I've graduated from high school*?

He finally got her out of his trunk and dumped his stupid crap in there instead and then stood in front of her and told her he was taking her to a bus station. She then began to cry, and the next thing our poor gentleman knew, she was riding shot-gun and messing with the radio. *And having to pee every fucking ten minutes.* Brookline never felt so fucking far.

Showing up with a seventeen-year-old girl wearing a skin-tight tank top emblazed with the two words—no thirty-something girlfriend wants to see emblazed on the girl standing at your side—*Hot Stuff* is not a good thing. It will cause a lot of problems, and considering candle light, Bill Evans, and poached salmon were waiting—preying on the table of our man's gorgeous nineteenth-century dining room—well, all our man could say to himself was, *I'm so screwed.* That was what our man said on the inside, and as for our man on the outside, it did not help that he had a boner, because his trunk girl kept on fiddling with his dick as he drove.

Looking back, this was probably the funniest moment of our man's whole experience with trunk girl (and his then girlfriend for that matter). But to understand why he thought it was so funny, you have to understand his girlfriend at the time. She was so fucking dry and uptight and rigid, and she just wanted wanted wanted. She would sit in his bed with some stupid-supposed-to-be-sexy pajamas and wear these glasses, and she would have all of her make-up off, and she would be flipping through catalogs. And our man would walk into the bedroom naked, and the first thing she would say to him was *Honey, do you think this is cute? Honey? Or, do you think it's too...oh, I don't know...what do you think?* However, while she's soliciting taste approval he's thinking, *get your ass in the air and let's be man and woman.* But the sight of her wearing bedclothes that looked just like the bedclothes in her catalogs always made him feel hollow, and his flickering want to enter her quickly shifted to hostility, and so he would give her the opinion she wanted. He would take the catalog from her, look at the queried item, and then tell her that she was too fat to wear something like that. She then would get up and sit in the bathroom until she was sure our man was sound asleep.

This routine between the two had been going on for some time, and when our man walked in with trunk girl, he made the quick decision to let it ride. He enjoyed the whole scene. She threw the dinner at him, swore a great deal, and turned fuchsia. And for the first time, she wasn't so dry, and our man found himself really wanting her. She flew out of his house and never—ever did she fly back in.

Trunk girl quickly became house mouse. She just sort of scuttled to one of the floors of our gentleman's old keep and lived. She would appear at feeding times, and she would sometimes play some of her music, or sometimes she would ask for the tiniest amounts of money. He always wondered what one does with ten dollars.

Late at night, she would sometimes crawl into his bed and rub against our man, and he would hold her, but he was still held at bay. This did not bug him much, because he had found some regular sex from a biologist across the river in Cambridge. He did not even have a tag name for this girl, though sometimes he did refer to her in his thoughts as *Regular*.

It was an amazing late fall night. The sky was deep blue, and our man was in his amber-colored study. He was trying to tie up a big Vietnam deal and was enjoying work and his desk. His old fireplace was just backing up enough to make him feel important. If he had had a good cigar at the moment, he would have smoked it. When she came in, he was a little caught off guard. Little house mouse did not just come in—let alone our man's sacred den. No, house mouse met him in the kitchen or dining room, or sometimes she would watch television with him and yes, she sometimes would crawl into his bed. However, she never did just come in.

Our gentleman turned to her and said, *well well.* And she said she had something she wanted to discuss. This was also strange. House mouse just talked. Never did she pre-announce that she was going to. Our man replied, *okay what?* Then she plainly said, *I want to go to college, and I want you to send me.*

Our man was surprised. He had no clue what to say or do. As for admission girl, she just stood in front of him wearing a pair of pink terry cloth sweat pants and a tight t-shirt that said USA. Her hair was in this big, sort of exploding up-do. Then after a long silence, she said, *I really want to dooooo this.* He rubbed his chin and scanned his position. He did have tons of money, and he did not have a wife or kids. He owned his house and car and place on the Cape. He knew it wouldn't hurt him *there.* But there was something that felt creepy to our man about sending a girl to college. Soon after their initial encounter in his den, he was driving admission girl all over New England touring schools and helping her fill out the most annoying and tedious applications he had ever seen in his life. Looking back on this time, our man did make a rather deep note of admission girl, because it was one of the few times in his life that he had something pegged all wrong. It seemed, after he had made way too many calls to her high school (which irritated him to the point of near madness), his little admission girl did quite, no very, well in high school. So well, in fact, that they were actually able to use academic excellence as a criterion for their school shopping. The night she had told him that she wanted to go to college, our man struggled not to laugh in her presence, as he felt that what she wanted was awesomely unreachable, as surely he felt her intelligence and education level to be very low and poor.

College girl decided on Williams in Williamstown, MA. He was a little uneasy about her choice. Williams was nearly the purest preppy enclave on earth—and well, our man would not exactly peg his girl as preppy. Trampy, trashy, cheap, tacky, sexy—yes. Preppie—no. Also, and he hated admitting this—even now—he was more than a little bummed she did not pick a school in town (as the Greater Boston Metro area had countless colleges). But no, she picked Williams, and he dropped her off there. The trip was more than just a little weird. They bought crap for her dorm room. He set up an open account at the school's bookstore for her. He set up a very generous account at the local bank. He also bought her a bicycle, and while he didn't tell her, he was considering—if she did well—maybe getting her a car. At the end of Incoming Freshman Weekend, college girl and our man shared a quiet, uneasy surf and turf dinner, and he walked her back to her dorm. He felt weird kissing her there—around so many other college girls with their crying parents. Lastly, he touched her shoulder and said goodbye and loads of other things like *anything at all just call.*

Our man drove home the most confused man on the planet.

Her four years at Williams were almost mundane. There were lots of calls with tearful questions regarding her school work, and sometimes he swore she just wanted to talk to him. However, with college girl, he could never really tell. She came home to him and stayed with him for every holiday and every summer, and she, and she, and she *changed a lot.*

First of all, changed girl smoked. A lot. Countless times he yelled at her for sneaking cigarettes in her bedroom (a very forbidden act). He finally then had a smoking gazebo built for her in the backyard, so she would be able to smoke when it was raining. Changed girl also now sported a bob. The shortness was not what really shocked him when she came home at the end of her first year at Williams. It was the fact that her bob was brown (and not the crispy, butter blonde she self-dyed perpetually in the third-floor, hallway bathroom). It was smooth too. Changed girl also now wore windbreakers and sweaters and silver-craft jewelry. Changed girl no longer wore make-up, which oddly made her look older and younger at once. It was not just the appearance that changed on changed girl.

She began to tell our gentleman about wine and jazz and Vietnam. And it was clear (and these were her very words) to our man how she felt about his place in all this: she informed him that he was, point in fact, *a developing-world rapist.* This made our man furious—and then her even more furious—because he would (after being referred to as a *rapist*) then point out that even after all this, not once, had he fucked her. *Not once*!

After graduation, she came home to him. She had resettled into his home. On one rainy night, they both found themselves alone together. There was so much thunder and lightning that he could no longer bear seeing her out there smoking in his little smoking gazebo that he had built for her. He called her inside and promised she could smoke her heart out inside. She came in. They were sitting in his living room. He was reading *The Wall Street Journal* wearing most of his suit—just not the coat. She was curled up on the couch and smoking. Then it all happened. He lowered his newspaper and asked her if she wanted anything from the kitchen. He wanted something from the kitchen, and so he was asking her if she wanted anything from the kitchen. She then sighed and stood up. He put his paper all the way down and sat up a bit. (This instinct would haunt him even now.) Our man had the sudden intense want or need to have his suit on all the way.

She walked towards him. *You know I've graduated*, she said. Our man sort of smiled and told her that he was really proud of her. *You know you can have me now*, she said. Our man shut his eyes, and if at that moment he could have shut more, he would have. *I can have you now?* He returned with quiet horror. *Yeah, you can have me now*, she returned like a fucking ping pong. Our man looked away. He looked away, because he was so angry that if he did not, he surely would have struck her. *So*, he began with a very weak voice, *so that is what is all was? I sent you to school, and now you are paying me back? Was this a deal? Was this all it was a motherfucking deal? So all those nights...years... were just a scam to get you through college, and now I can have you, and now you will pay me...with you*?

He then slumped on the arm of his favorite chair and felt the saliva evaporate from his opened mouth. She remained still, standing in front of him. *You fucking bitch*, he said. She then then turned her face partially away. Her eyes though remained locked on his. *No*, she finally said. *No*? he asked. *NO*, she emphatically returned. *Then what darling, what was all this about?* he asked, completely furious.

Our man sat completely still for just a second, long enough to take it all in. He then stood up. He stood up so strongly that he almost fell as soon as he stood. *You white trash piece of shit*, was his opener. The saliva returned as he screamed, and by the time he was standing in the doorway of her bedroom, he could feel it foam and fly out of his mouth as she just silently packed her things. His rant never ceased—even as she loaded the Volkswagen he had purchased for her as a graduation present. She never said a word. He never saw or heard from her again.

And now? Now our gentleman, our developer, is in a hotel in Thailand pounding out all of this garbage, all of this history, on his laptop. He can hear his two bored prostitutes chatting on his bed and snorting cocaine. *I am still so angry and confused. Everywhere I find myself looking for another grocery store girl, and yet, never before in my life have I been more terrified of them.*

The Maury Story (Lizzie)

"Have I got a story for you guys," said Roy with a sort of *Ho Ho Ho* joy. His whole head was bright red. His hair and whiskers were snow white, and his largess, though strong and round, only rose to five foot three inches.

Lizzie, already pretty buzzed, was only loosely listening. Her head was bobbing to music that was playing in another room. "Seth, will you get me one too," Lizzie blurted.

Seth then handed Roy (our interrupted story teller) a beer, and then Roy handed it to Lizzie. Roy then eyed his small halo of listeners and smiled like a sleeping dog as Lizzie opened her bottle and took a drink. She was completely oblivious to the fact that she was holding up a story that Roy wanted to tell and that others in the kitchen wanted to hear. Roy, however, was not upset. His countenance remained peaceful; he was a soul who took others' flaws with profound patience.

"Now, I know you guys will never believe this story, but I swear to you that everything I tell you is absolutely true." Roy then surveyed his audience. Everyone was standing around the kitchen counter, and they were all completely silent.

"So, I had this buddy named Maury...."

"Maury who?" asked Seth with both authority and seniority. Seth had known Roy the longest of the group, and in this case *longest* meant many, many years, and it was strongly felt by the tone of Seth's voice that if this account was to be taken as the complete truth, then Seth must also have known the man presented in Roy's story. It is also important to note that these sorts of clerical issues were always being brought up by Seth.

Roy rose his hand with his soft, usual, and kind smile.

"Who is he?" demanded Seth with a barely perceptible slur.

"This guy Maury was a pretty serious alcoholic. I mean, this guy was one of those intense types." Roy then simulated chugging from an invisible bottle. It was clear Roy was not going to stop his story to satisfy Seth's demanding need for historical bookkeeping.

"Maury was a nice guy. A quiet guy. I first met him when I was a bartender—the first time I was a bartender—back when I was married. Well anyway, this Maury guy had no good luck. You could just tell by the way his god-awful brown suit hung on him that nothing good ever happened to Maury. But the guy was a nice guy.

"He came in every night, and every night he would order a bottle of Bud Light with a shot of house whiskey. A bottle and a shot, and a bottle and a shot, and a bottle and a shot, all night 'till closing.

"We would sometimes talk on slower, quieter nights, because this guy was pretty quiet. He communicated a great deal with sighs and listening. Strange breed...but true."

"What does that mean?" Lizzie asked.

"Looking down. Looking away. Nodding one's head. Pulling the label off one's beer...all these things are the listener's ways of telling you who they are. Like one night when I was talking about my pregnant wife and how she was planning on quitting her job, because it would be our third baby, and that she didn't make enough money to cover day care for three...and how all this meant I had to find a job that had medical insurance, and leaving the bar felt like leaving life (this was all said in an almost pre-recorded tone, partially because just about all of Roy's stories managed to include some gripe as to how and why his ex-wife had truly ruined him and partially because Roy had turned his past into a sort of rhythmic chant with the sincere hope that somehow he would come to a kind of realization or enlightenment).

"Anyway," said Roy, "as I talked crap, Maury

kept on coughing and spinning his shot glass.... I knew right then and there that Maury did not have a wife or kids, and this fact bummed him out.

"Furthermore, I could see that this Maury character never got laid."

"How? I mean how could you get all that from his coughing and spinning?" Lizzie asked while lighting a cigarette.

"Then a whole year went by," continued Roy—completely ignoring Lizzie's question. "A whole year went by that I did not see Maury. And the funny thing was that I didn't miss him or even remember him until he walked in the bar...."

At this point, Roy ceased storytelling and began to hug and greet Brian. Brian had just entered. He was wearing a very thick, Irish wool sweater, and his shoes and jeans were wet with snow.

Brian warmly greeted everybody. He smelled strongly of cologne. He kissed Lizzie on her cheek and took one of her cigarettes without asking. Everyone then resettled like birds in a nest, and Roy continued.

"Maury walked in, and while it was hard at the time for one to have imagined it possible...Maury appeared ten times shittier...and quieter. (There was then a long pause—Roy had spilled his beer, and there was a hasty—but thorough clean-up.) As it turned out, Maury had sobered up. He went to AA—the whole nine yards. And jeezus...the man looked completely lifeless.

"Lifeless.... I'm not even sure if 'lifeless'

encompassed the man that shuffled into the bar and plunked down. I was ready with his shot and bottle, and he rose his puffy hand and said, 'Just a coke. I'm just drinking the soft stuff now.'

"I chuckled, downed the shot, and then handed the guy a coke.

"This went on for weeks—months. Every night he would come in wearing the same awful, I mean jeezus, just awful brown suit looking soggier and soggier and drinking a half dozen or so cokes. Every once in a while, we would talk...but he had grown so quiet that only on the rarest of evenings would it be silent enough for us to talk. Slowly, I began to know the life of Maury. He was out of work—sold clothes wholesale. He was forty-two. The last girl he had truly known was in high school. Oddly enough though...the guy played the piano...that still kills me...the guy played the goddamned piano."

Lizzie's eyes drifted away from Roy and focused on Brian. Brian kept on trying to get Lizzie out of the room—out of the kitchen—and she was not budging. He then gave up and drifted away.

"Seth, want to hand me another beer?" Lizzie asked.

Seth ignored Lizzie. Lizzie's husband Jeff then went to the refrigerator and got her a bottle of beer.

"So, then what happened?" asked Seth with a scowl. Brian may have left, but an almost breathing jealousy had entered the kitchen. Seth's anger was so naked towards Lizzie that she felt an almost militant attention towards Roy and his story enter her body.

It was as if her whole life would implode if she were to do anything besides stay in that kitchen and listen to Roy's story.

"It was not a quiet night when Maury's world completely exploded," began Roy with his soft rasp of a voice. "At first he did order his pop...but he...but the damn man looked so bad he made me truly afraid to be human. I asked him, as usual, how things were going, and instead of shrugging, he pinched his eyes with a trembling hand.

"'Ahh damn,' said Maury, 'I'll take a beer and a shot.' Now, Seth will know exactly what I did. In fact, it's one of most profound codes of honor for a bartender."

"What did you do?" asked Jeff, Lizzie's husband.

"He gave him a shot and a beer," quite seriously answered Seth. (Seth was also a bartender.)

"Exactly," beamed Roy. But his beam was precisely warm—not excited or proud. "I handed him several shots and beers that night, and Maury got loaded. *I mean loaded.* And for the first time, I can remember at least, he took off his awful brown coat and tie. It was as if he needed more room to invite the kind of drunk he wanted to meet."

"For the next couple of weeks, Maury came in each night and got seriously drunk. But you know, there was something different about him. It wasn't actually until a full month had gone by that I finally queried him about this subtle—yet profound change I was sensing in him."

"What was it?" asked Lizzie's husband, Jeff.

Roy nodded gently to Lizzie's husband. "He said, 'Roy, I actually sat down and put together a new resume and well, I think I nailed a job. I also, well, I also have been talking to this girl. Actually, I've been talking to all the girls I encounter. I don't know any of them yet...but before...before I wouldn't even talk to them.'

"You can all imagine my surprise," said Roy. "I mean, jeezus, this Maury guy took loser to a whole new level...but somehow there was a glimpse of shine in old Maury's face."

"Was he still drinking just as heavily?" asked Lizzie's husband.

"Like you wouldn't believe!" exclaimed Roy. "In fact, he was even starting to snort cocaine! Honest to god! One night, after hours, we were—you know—having a beer together, and low and behold, he offered me some coke! Jeezus, coke."

Roy's voice, for the first time, grew grave, "It was actually on that night, the coke night, that Maury dropped the bomb. Maury had finally landed a job! He was hired as the Misses and Juniors department manager at the brand-new Lord and Taylor. It also was revealed that Maury had graduated from talking to chicks to asking them out. The guy was dating... *the guy was dating.* Maury was going on real, live dates. Jeezus, I almost died where I stood that night. Blow me down."

Lizzie's husband kept everyone in fresh beers with an unimaginable silence and timeliness. Unlike Lizzie, he was impeccably polite. After Roy had said,

"Blow me down," Lizzie was thunderstruck with an almost choking despair. She did not know why. She was struggling to hide the fact that her eyes were tearing up.

"Yeah...but do you really know if these chicks even existed? Or even the gig at Lord and Taylor?" observed Seth the Observant.

Roy began to nod his head sympathetically. "First off, he began to bring some of the girls into the bar. And man, total hotties. Babes."

"Would he still get just as loaded?" Lizzie asked.

"Absolutely!" chortled Roy.

"Would his dates get just as loaded?" asked Lizzie's husband.

Roy darkened a bit then answered. "No. I mean, yeah, sure, some of the girls would get loaded. But not Maury, or you know, *professionally* loaded. No, they were really beautiful, really amazing girls. They were all *daughters* if you know what I mean."

"What was Maury like at this point?" Lizzie asked.

"Ahh Jeez," began Roy. He even scratched his head and bent his knee, and this made Lizzie smile wide, and then he winked at her. Roy had seen the despair touch Lizzie, and from there on out he was going to take the mood up a bit and make a little more fun of everything.

"He wasn't so quiet I guess...yeah...Maury now talked and laughed. He never did any of that before. But there was something about the new Maury that made you happy for him—not jealous or even confused. The new, successful, hard-drinking Maury had a sort of dark luck about him...but I mainly remember that Maury had something about him that just drew you in. It's just so hard to nail down. And this is important. It's important, because Maury was not stopping at dates with real girls and walking the floor of a fancy department store—oh, and I almost forgot—dumpy, soggy, bad, brown suit Maury was no longer. Gradually, through money and a steep discount at Lord and Taylor's, no doubt, Maury became the man with a million—if you know what I mean. Sometimes I would just stare at the new Maury...flabbergasted...completely flabbergasted!"

"And he is still getting just as wasted? Nightly?" asked Lizzie's husband with a laughing shrill voice.

"Like you would not believe. It seemed for Maury the more he drank, the better his life became. The chicks were getting increasingly more beautiful and even more sincere. His grooming and carriage were becoming so fine that noticeable intimidation was radiating from the other patrons at the bar."

"Come on, Roy," interjected Seth, "The guy just managed a dozen bimbos at the mall." It was clear at this point to everyone in the kitchen, but most especially Lizzie, that Seth was not going to be happy for the rest of the night.

"No, no, that's what I was trying to get at," said Roy with a patient, knowing grin. "You see, the damnedest thing happened—and you know, (Roy then particularly focused on Seth) I would have never believed Maury had I not had outside source confirmation. Well, it seems that when Lord and Taylor's bought the Bon White department store, they asked Mr. and Mrs. White, the owners of Bon White, to stay on and run the store as Lord and Taylor's. Lord and Taylor's thought keeping the Whites would retain at least some of the grand old Bon White feeling."

"Okay, so listen to this," continued Roy, "As it turns out, all along, old Mr. White was gay. Honest to god. And I guess Mrs. White had just had it. And when the old gal had just had it, she found herself alone with Maury in his tiny, windowless office. So anyway, as poor old Mrs. White is having at it with some tears, old Maury produces a bottle of *Dewars* from his desk drawer. Next thing you know, Mr. White out...Maury in. Honest to god."

"Did they get together?" Lizzie asked laughing.

"No, according to Maury they just sat in his office and proceeded to get hammered—big time. And after they drained his office bar, they went out to his car and drained his car bar, and then they went to his apartment, and they drained his apartment bar. So, then they got the idea to eat. All Maury could think to do was order pizza. He was beginning to already get nervous about the outcome of all this, and Maury was shitting bricks that presenting *thee* Mrs. White with a pizza was going to be the end of Maury. So, here's Maury just wasted with his seventy-something...."

"Seventy-something?" Lizzie shrieked.

Roy twinkled his eyes sublimely towards Lizzie. "Didn't I mention that?" laughed Roy, "*Thee* Mrs. White was a silver Grande Dame if there ever was one.

"So, anyway Mrs. White was starving and in dire need. The pizza came. Both Maury and Mrs. White finished the large with everything and then calm. Maury had managed to stagger to the couch and even turn on the television. However, Mrs. White found herself in the most brutal pass-out position of the head on its side flat on the table. Jeezus, that is the most painful waking position ever—I assure you.

"So, anyway, both Maury and Mrs. White remained passed out for around an hour or two and then—and then—the barfing began!" howled Roy. "Maury described it as being the most horrifying moment of his life. It opened, he said, with the loudest, sharpest burp he had ever heard. Startled, Maury looked over the back of the couch towards the dining area only to find Mrs. White tossing her chair to the ground while attempting a Frankenstein-like stagger towards nowhere, and before Maury could gather his wits, an enormous fall of gold-colored vomit came out of her mouth. Maury found himself unable to move. Then before Maury's brain could truly assist his eyes, the poor old lady was stumbling all over his apartment puking. She was pulling out kitchen drawers, dragging down end tables, falling over and crushing lit lamps—all the while vomiting everywhere. Maury had never seen so much puke. The poor guy was in shock. He was sure old Mrs.

White was going to die. But he didn't part from his couch, and he admitted there truly was so much vomit that he truly *did not* want to leave his couch. His couch had become a life raft in a sea of old lady puke.

"Finally, with crazy eyes and a still impeccable, silver beehive, Mrs. White found her way to the couch. There she faced Maury and paused, and Maury prayed that Mrs. White was going to collapse. However, Maury was an experienced drunk, and he knew with her slowly arching back and bulging eyes that it was going to come. Almost as quickly as he realized what was to occur, a three-foot torrent of vomit arched out of her mouth directly onto Maury and his burgundy velour vessel.

"Then, as if Mrs. White had merely been possessed and not poisoned, her mouth closed and her eyes returned to their sockets. Her cheeks returned to pale blue versus green red, and her spine settled back into a soft hunch. Mrs. White then retrieved her pocketbook and coat and walked out the door, taking great care not to step in any of her sick.

"But you know Mrs. White really was a Grande Dame. The next day, not only was she at work, but she also appeared as polished and solid as ever. The same, however, could not be said for poor Maury. It was not booze or lack thereof that was giving him the shakes that morning; it was facing Mrs. White. He was sure he was doomed...and sure enough, the moment Maury entered his office, a memo was waiting for him. He was to meet with Mrs. White at precisely two p.m.

"As if by a miracle, however, Maury had found an undrained thermos full of vodka underneath a pile of mistagged jackets. So, at least he didn't have to face her without a little preferred blood.

"She was neither warm nor cold with him. Maury scanned her face with all his might and nowhere could he see the night they had shared. Nowhere. Mrs. White told him to wait a moment alone. When she returned, she was accompanied by a youngish woman in a suit. The woman was a corporate H.R. person. Mrs. White had arranged Maury a job with corporate Lord and Taylor's. The pay would be nearly five times what he was making. He would be traveling the world buying textiles for a new in-house clothing and home decor venture. And he would be professionally moved—all expenses paid—*the next day* to New York City. Say your good-byes, Maury. Maury, say your good-byes.

"As you can imagine, his last night at the bar was awesome. Man, Lord and Taylor's had the hottest chicks ever...and they all came...and they all were huggers. I actually think I saw God that night. We partied 'till dawn. A beer with a shot. Bam! A beer with a shot. Bam! All night."

A perceptible sheet of mist drifted over Roy's face, and everyone in the kitchen knew the story, the Maury story had ended. Lizzie wanted desperately to know what had become of Maury—*what was Maury doing now*? *Was his badness still turning into goodness? Was his simultaneous escalation of drinking and success now reaching dizzying heights?* These were things Lizzie really wanted to know.

For the duration of the party, Lizzie continued to light Seth's cigarettes, because he could not, because he was holding and gently stroking soft, purring jealousy. Lizzie did manage to steal a little kiss and grope from Brian and then went home and curled warmly around her husband.

Cold Hearted Woman (Annette)

Annette felt that she had forgiven quite enough to prove that she was forgiving. However, there came a time when she did not want to forgive, and when that time did come, Annette realized that while it was forgivable to do all sorts of terrible things, to not forgive was, for many, unforgivable.

Annette was fairly ordinary excepting for a loveliness and orderliness that was seen by most as fairly uncommon. Otherwise, her profession of managing a small, high-end antique store owned by her aunt, her marriage to an attorney specializing in tax evasion cases, her three-bedroom townhouse, and her friends and relatives were all ordinary, even in the cases of extreme this and odd that. The aunt that owned the antique store was her mother's sister and was somewhat rich and somewhat of a drunk.

Annette's mother in a kind of dignified, dividing way never drank alcohol and married a service manager at an auto dealership that provided for Annette's family a consistent and basic life of well and good and fine with the occasional hiccup. There were bad and good hiccups like the time they all went to Hawaii for Easter or the time when Annette's mother was terribly ill, and Annette had to withdraw from college to pay the mounting medical bills. When Annette's mother did become well, Annette had already found herself finely suited in a job working for her aunt, so college seemed unnecessary. Annette had an older sister who was married right out of high school to her older, divorced boyfriend. They now had three children and lived in a townhouse in the same gated community as Annette and her new husband. It took many months and the arrival of a terribly happy baby boy for Annette to forgive her sister's older, previously divorced husband for stealing her sister's youth and future. Annette's marriage came about in a very dignified and dividing way, as they met at the country club where her wealthy aunt socialized and drank and talked a great deal at a very great volume. He was someone's son, and he immediately admired Annette. He fell in love with her because of her ordinariness and her uncommon beauty and order. Annette had perfect posture, conservatively covered large bosoms, slim ankles, wondrously drawn eyes, and a speech style that could be compared to a quiet piano. Annette liked him fine. Annette's older sister thought he was an asshole, Annette's mother said that if she liked him then that was all that mattered, and Annette's father felt he was an insecure man. When she was sober, Annette's aunt slash employer thought that Annette's husband was a good man deep down inside. When she was drunk, Annette's aunt varied in her estimations: sometimes he was an asshole, sometimes he was hot, and sometimes he was a true-blue husband type. As for Annette's friends, most felt that he was cool or cute or nice.

Upon the arrival of Annette's sister's third child, their mother grew ill again. These were darker times, as Annette's father had been laid off due to lackluster sales at the auto dealership, and Annette's older sister could not help, as they were now bless-burdened with a brand new mouth. During this time, Annette's aunt seemed to be drinking heavier than ever and seemed to be even more varied in her opinions regarding just about everyone she and Annette knew and loved. Luckily, Annette and her husband had kept their life modest and harmoniously in step with their careers, and while it would be a strain to help Annette's family with the mounting medical bills, it would not be enough to wreck or ruin them. However, it was a strain.

Annette was uncommonly orderly, and being uncommonly orderly meant that Annette had an almost supernatural eyesight when it came to the first, nearly imperceptible signs of disorder. Annette had to leave work at five to pick her mother up from the hospital, feed her mother, tidy up her parent's house, and then pick up some of her mother's prescriptions. When it was Annette's turn for these duties, it was agreed that her aunt would mind the antique store until Annette's return, which was usually around eight-thirty in the evening. Annette would then tidy up the store, close out the register, do the bookkeeping, close up the store, and then drop off the day's take at the bank before returning home. This day was extraordinary, for when Annette returned to the store, Annette found not only her aunt there (drinking of course) but her husband as well. Now, it was certainly not unusual for Annette to find her aunt drinking on the job, but it was nearly faint-worthy to see her husband drinking with her. In fact, Annette could not remember any time that the two had fraternized alone. Now, surely her country-clubby raised husband was confident and frequent with drinking alcohol, however, seeing him drinking and chatting lively with her drinking and shouting lively aunt in a high-end antique store was almost repulsive in its too forceful element-of-surprisiness.

Once Annette internally calmed herself from the spectacle, she managed to click off a few notes of *what are you doing here*. The drinking two set down their drinks, and her husband explained that he had simply stopped in to say hello. This caused a very subtle and hardly noticeable eyebrow raise on Annette's terribly handsome face, as Tuesdays were always pick up mother days, and surely he knew this. "But maybe, but maybe he forgot, maybe he is simply too overworked to keep such records," thought Annette as she tidied up the store and prepared it for closing under the din of florid conversation and clinking. It seemed that Annette's aunt was compelled (almost compulsively) to make many, many toasts that evening.

After Annette had finished closing the store, she climbed into her car, and she kissed her husband lightly on the lips as he leaned deeply through the window of her car. "See you back at home?" she asked.

"I thought we should go out for dinner," he said as he returned to standing.

"I already made us some dinner this morning. It is in the refrigerator," Annette returned.

"But I want to go out," he said.

"It's Tuesday...I'm very tired," she sighed.

"But I don't want to go home yet," he said.

"Fine," she said.

She followed her husband through town. He led her to his favorite restaurant. It was billed as being *Polynesian*, but it was really heavily westernized Chinese with the bulk of the menu consisting of appetizers and long-named cocktails. The restaurant was very dark and decorated in World War II Hawaiian fantasy. It was packed with pickled country clubbers, lawyers, nurses, and college students aspiring to be country clubbers, lawyers, and nurses. Annette wanted desperately to be at home and to eat the dinner she had made that morning which was chickeny with a little bit of noodle and vegetable. Annette wanted to be out of her pantyhose and heels and in some lounge clothes that, although felt like sweatpants, were lovely, taupe, and refined. She wanted to admire her impeccably groomed feet crossed over her gray leather ottoman. She wanted a tidy peace.

Her husband chatted animatedly about work and his goals in life and what he thought of the news of the day and who was sitting where at the restaurant and what his opinions were regarding said person. And as he spun his words and ideas along with dipping countless deep-fried shapes into little pots of sticky, orange-colored fluid and downing gin and tonic after gin and tonic, Annette felt as though she was going to have an unhappiness induced seizure, as truly the room was spinning. She simply refused to enjoy or accept being at that loud, dark restaurant with her ever increasingly loud and dark husband.

It was not that Annette was opposed to Polynesian restaurants or even pickled people. It also was not that Annette was down on her husband's dreams and observations. It was that she was simply tired. It was Tuesday, and on Tuesdays, she was extraordinarily tired. On Tuesdays, Annette had learned that if she made a mild chicken dinner in the morning and went straight home after work and put on some high-end loungewear, then Tuesdays could have a kind of goodness. Tuesdays could have a happy place in her life like a rainy day can have a happy place in nature, and usually, her husband knew this, and she thought he had admired and understood how she had managed to organize Tuesdays.

But today, this Tuesday was going terribly wrong, and this created a sense of dread for Annette. *Something was slipping away. Something was loosening.* These would be the last two lines Annette would think to herself before she opened her legs for her husband that night and then fell deeply asleep.

Wednesday was normal.

Thursday began and rolled convincingly normally until Annette came home. Thursdays were the one day Annette's aunt promised to stay sober enough to allow Annette to be home by six in the evening. Every other day barring Sundays (as the store was closed on Sunday), Annette did not get off work until nine thirty or so depending on how long it took to lock up and do the day's bookkeeping. Thursdays were joyous days for Annette, as she could feel like a friend or wife or sister on those days. Every other day, she was a waterwheel: cooking, cleaning, shopping, working, listening, opening her legs, and sleeping. But on Thursdays, she could be subjective and experience things like crabby, silly, funny, angry, judgmental, concerned, and even tipsy.

This Thursday, however, was odd. When Annette entered her home, anxious to kiss her husband's neck and call out to those she loved, she found a dark and silent house. Normally, her husband was standing in the garage, timing his arrival nearly perfectly with hers. Or, her husband was already inside wearing shorts and a t-shirt and bare feet. Or, her husband was drinking a beer and watching the local news. This Thursday, however, the house was dark and silent, which was doubly startling, as her husband's car was indeed in its spot in the garage.

Before allowing herself to give over to panic, Annette paced the house turning on lights and calling out to her husband. There was still no answer. Again, in an effort not to worry, Annette carried on as if he were there (as he was normally there on Thursdays) and proceeded to change into jeans, thong sandals, and a linen tunic. "Perhaps he was out running," she thought, though did not believe, as her husband was never out running on Thursday. Monday, Tuesday, Wednesday, Friday maybe, but on Thursdays, he was always waiting for her.

"Hey, sis," said a mildly rattled Annette to her sister on the telephone.

"Hey girl," returned her sister. "Where are you?"

"I'm at home," said Annette with confusion. "Why?"

"Well, your husband is here, and I just assumed when I answered the door and saw him with a case of beer in his arms that you were literally like seconds away," answered Annette's older sister.

"He's at your house?" asked Annette.

"Yeah...isn't that weird?" returned her sister. "I never thought we were country club enough for him...he only hung out with us, I thought, because of you."

Normally, Sunday began with eleven a.m. service at her husband's childhood church then on to the country club for brunch with his family. Sunday dinner was usually at Annette's parent's house or sometimes her older sister's townhouse but nearly never at her house, as Annette and her new husband were not quite seen as mature enough to hold such an event. This was a convenient convention for Annette, as usually she was terribly worn out on Sunday and genuinely needed to float and follow. This Sunday, however, was unique, as her mother, father, and baby brother were all at a university hospital two hours out of town for the week. There at the university hospital, her mother was going to undergo a special, experimental treatment. Annette had very mixed feelings regarding this change, as on the one hand it signaled just how sick her mother really was; however, on the other hand, it gave Annette an unexpected evening of freedom. Annette could barely follow her husband's family's conversations at brunch, as she was already thinking about how she was going to spend her surprise income of time.

While walking through the parking lot of the country club, a friend of her husband came whizzing up to them in a golf cart. Her husband happily trotted up to his friends in the golf cart while Annette meekly let herself in the car. After around five or six minutes, Annette's husband joined her in the car and informed Annette that he had invited his friend and his girlfriend over for dinner. He suggested spaghetti as he pulled out of the parking lot.

For a few hours, Annette cleaned her townhouse and internally shouted at her husband; however, by the time she returned from the grocery store and found him listening to loud music of his high school days while drinking a beer, she softened and forgave him. She instantly recognized the need behind his oafishness (she saw he was perhaps missing his youth, his glory days), and in doing so, turned the other cheek and decided to give him the shirt (of freedom) he had stolen from her. It was Sunday after all. She would not only cook the very best dinner she could.

Company arrived. He was a friend of her husband's from high school. He was wealthy by blood and blood work, as he worked under his father at their family's enormous chicken operation. His girlfriend was a novelty at the country club, as she was a young emergency room doctor. Very few women of their set had jobs, let alone careers that held titles. She went to boarding school and college in England and medical school in America. She was currently a resident at the town's largest hospital. She had an English accent but was an American. Her father was a professor at the London School of Economics. Annette's husband would repeatedly tell Annette in private as they were getting more wine or more crackers that he found the doctor's accent, intelligence, and physique to be "wild," "sexy," "wow," and "cool." Annette was surprisingly fine with her husband's comments, as she agreed. Annette liked the young emergency doctor, as she was incredibly sharp and perhaps (Annette felt) a little on the mean side. Annette always liked women who were a little on the mean side. When Annette contemplated this, she always used it to explain why it was she stood by her flaky boss slash aunt. Her aunt was a little on the mean side, and somehow it was comforting to be near and bring glasses of wine and little bowls of oyster crackers to women who were a little mean. They would always say things like "thank you, dear," "isn't he an asshole?", and "where's the bathroom?". Women on the mean side were like very cold and very clear rivers to Annette—unlike women on the nice side who very often felt like warm, murky ponds to be around. Annette knew from her campfire girl days that one should never swim in or drink from stagnant water. The only problem that Annette was having with her thoughts on women was that she feared that she indeed ran a little on the nice side.

After their salads, her husband cleared everyone's plates away as Annette served up the spaghetti dinners in the dining room that opened up to a large television focused sitting area with large gray leather sofas and glass and metal coffee and end tables. When she placed the plate in front of everyone, her husband's old high school friend told her that it looked delicious and that he was excited to dig in. His girlfriend then said, "I never cook." Annette then took off her apron and sat down. She was about to take a bite when she noticed that her husband was pushing the spaghetti and bolognese sauce around his plate with his fork.

"This isn't the way it supposed to be," said Annette's husband. "There's no sauce, it's all thick and standing on top of the pasta."

"It's a recipe from the New York Times," said Annette in middle C.

"Well, then you messed up, because it is not even red. And I see carrots, and it is thick," complained Annette's husband. "It's all sticking to the noodles. Why didn't you put the sauce on top? Why did you mix it all up?"

"Well, I think it looks great," said her husband's friend.

"Well, I think it looks like shit," said her husband. "Netty, you know I like my spaghetti the way I make it with the red sauce and chopped tomatoes and the ground beef...it pours like a sauce...*spaghetti sauce*...this is all clumpy and thick and brown and why in the hell are there goddamned carrots and... is that celery? Why is there carrots and celery in this fucking sauce?"

Annette looked at her guests. They were both extremely uncomfortable. Luckily, the young doctor was still able to sip her wine during the storm—this comforted Annette greatly.

"Look, I think it looks delicious Annette. Thank you very much," nervously said her husband's friend.

"Delicious? Delicious? You think this crap looks delicious?" asked Annette's husband, now profoundly angered. He then grabbed the spaghetti bolognese up with a clawed hand and shoved it into Annette's awed mouth and face. She was wearing a navy-blue shift dress with tiny, nearly imperceptible white polka dots. She was wearing a pair of pearl earrings.

Annette remained seated at the table while her dinner guests quietly said goodbye and left. Her husband walked them out. When her husband returned, they did not speak a word. He proceeded to clean the kitchen, living room area where they had had pre-dinner cocktails and appetizers, and the dining room, including the light gray carpet that had been stained with the spaghetti. As he cleaned, Annette remained seated on her chair as though frozen into stone. She did not speak or move after he had pushed the food forcefully into her mouth. Her husband tried at first to talk to her, but then soon realized it was probably best to fall silent. After cleaning everything up, her husband then went to bed.

When he awoke on Monday morning, he found his wife still sitting at the dinner table, awake, and still covered in meat sauce. He knelt by her side and said that he was sorry. When he did, she said nothing. He then said, "Please, baby?"

Annette finally, without addressing her husband, rose from her seat at the table and retreated to the master bedroom.

While her husband was at work, Annette packed all of her belongings and went to her parent's house. Her parents were still out of town, and she was relieved of that. When her parents did return home, Annette gave very little details, only that her marriage was over. They remained remarkably quiet regarding this for a few weeks. However, after a few weeks, they began—including her older sister—including all of her friends—including her older sister's husband—to harp on her regarding forgiveness and her shame-filled, lovesick, forlorn, and unforgiven husband. Only her aunt seemed varied regarding the situation: sometimes she felt that Annette was "damn right," and sometimes she would yell adamantly across the antiques store "Annette, you got to forgive people. You just do." Finally, after two months, her friends and family grew almost hostile in their nearly constant confronting entreaties that Annette should forgive her husband.

"Annette, honey, I did not raise you to be like this," said her mother to her in a very weak and watered-down voice. "Baby, you've got to forgive. You've got to do what Jesus instructed...otherwise, God will not forgive you...baby, God will not forgive your transgressions if you do not forgive the transgressions of others."

"But mother, I do not want to forgive him," answered Annette.

"But baby, think of yourself...forgiveness is really about setting yourself free, baby," said her mother.

"But I am free," replied Annette, "and as long as I do not forgive him, I will remain free. Besides, if your brand of forgiveness is really about self-consideration, then shouldn't I follow my heartfelt desire in that I do not want to forgive him?"

"No baby, I mean free of your anger. Baby, by forgiving him you will be free of your anger...you can move on, baby," said her mother.

"But I'm not angry anymore. There is no longer any anger that I need to be free of. My anger drifted away with time," answered Annette.

"Well, honey, if you're no longer angry, then why don't you forgive him?" asked her mother with a little bit of cough.

"Because if I forgive him, then he will think I mean to return to him for which I do not want to. Besides, I do not, in fact, forgive him. And even more so, I do not ever want to forgive him. If I forgive him, I will no longer be free. Forgiving someone bonds you to them forever, and I do not want to be bound to him forever," answered Annette. "Forgiveness is a promise, and whenever you make a promise to someone, you are always bound and never free, because your sole options are either being a good promiser or being a bad promiser, so I do not want to make any promises. Right now, I am pristinely free and under no burdens. Let him carry the burden of his actions. I do not want to take part in his transgressions. I am tired of taking part in his transgressions."

"Oh baby, you're talking in circles. Forgiving your husband does not mean you have to get back together with him. It just means that you no longer harbor any bad feelings towards him. It just means you no longer judge him by what he did," said her mother.

"Mom, I do not want to quarrel with you. *But.* But I do not agree with what forgiveness means to you. It is natural and protecting for me to have bad feelings regarding what he did. I believe people suffer when they have bad feelings about being the victim—when they feel that the offense was somehow their fault or that they deserved it—or worse, they feel shame for having been violated. However, I do not suffer such. I know I did not deserve what he did. Secondly, it seems Mother Nature most definitely wants us to judge others by what they do. Otherwise, we would let mountain lions near our campfire, we would still be trying to play with rattle snakes, or we would remain married to dangerous husbands. I think that today the word forgiveness has no real meaning, and while I know Jesus spoke of turning the other cheek, I am not so sure he would have made that call the night my husband assaulted me. I want to be safe and free. And while I know...I can see it in your eyes...that he did not really *hurt* me not *physically*...the signs were loud and clear that that was where things were heading. Mother, I wish no harm on my husband. However, I do not want to forgive him. I just don't, and it feels incredibly natural and wholesome not to want to," resolutely, though gently, returned Annette.

Annette's mother's face grew grimly hard. "Well then, Annette, God will not forgive you."

Annette then softly sighed and kissed her

mother lightly on the forehead. “I suppose then, mother, that God and I are now in the same boat.”

Calling Gwen
(Gwen)

You just cannot fully imagine all that comes into play when you call Gwen. First off, you are going to call her. *Everybody does*, but understand that calling Gwen is not going to be easy or comfortable.

Right off the bat, know that every time you call Gwen, she will make you regret it. She manages to do this with a myriad of techniques. Her most common technique is to be tired. She will listlessly say, "Hello" when she answers, but that's only after she opens with, "Who is this?" So, her fatigued *hello* feels personal. After her listless *hello*, know that you will only be allowed a brief volley of *hi*. Then quickly she will hint that her tired *hello* was real and that you are bothering her a little. Some typical Gwenisms: "I'm fine, just a little tired," "I was just about to brush my teeth," or "I'd like to get stuff done, but I keep getting interrupted." All of these Gwenisms will make you suddenly self-conscious—will make you feel like an intruder. The normal, natural reaction will, of course, be to retreat. These are some normal and completely understandable retreats: "Oh, I'm sorry...do you want me to go?", "I just wanted to say a quick hello," and "Yeah, it's late for me too. I just wanted to return your call." Now, the last retreat can only be used if Gwen did indeed call you previously.

Gwen does call previously; indeed, that is her favorite and most common form of communication. She will leave all sorts of quiet, sincere messages at all sorts of terrible times. These messages will be tender and sincere and sad. You will feel a strange twinge of being loved, and being cruel for not answering her clearly much wanted telephone conversation. She likes to call at ten or eleven in the evening on Saturday night, at seven in the evening on Sunday, and at nine-thirty in the evening on Thursday. I have never answered the telephone in my entire life at those times on those days, and I believe I have been prudent in this policy, and really when tackling the whole messy issue of calling Gwen, I heartily suggest that you too stick to your guns and refuse to pick up. Now, I suppose that you are wondering why I sound so adamant regarding the issue of not picking up the phone when Gwen calls me during blackout times—well, the reason is obvious—I have picked up before, and it proved disastrous.

As I said earlier, Gwen leaves these tender,

desperate messages that make you feel like a terrible person for not picking up. While you most likely will call her back as soon as you can, calling Gwen is just awful, so you will experiment with picking up the phone when she calls at impossible times like eleven at night on Saturday. First off, know she will be sober when she calls, which will not in any way mesh with your dignified and well deserved Saturday evening buzz. Secondly, know she will be unhappy about something yet will argue with every single suggestion you offer that might solve her problem. And trust me, as every single suggestion you are offering her is getting rebuffed, you will watch your friends come up to you and mouth the words *I'll talk to you tomorrow*. And then your once friend and music filled night becomes a buzz-killing, long distance, unhappy conversation. I've even lost dates to Gwen's calls. And this pains me, because life is hard and lonely, and we need beer on Saturdays along with friends and sometimes lovers. And really, you really—truly—must know that this has happened to me (more than once—because I am not good at learning lessons), and it will happen to you if you answer the phone when Gwen calls on an absurd time, and remember that is the only time she calls. Which brings us back to the fact that you cannot, must not, answer the phone when Gwen calls. You will indeed listen to her message. This will ignite a pressing need to call her back at a more reasonable time and day like Tuesday evening around eight when you are sober, and your friends are sober, and everything in the world is folding laundry, watching television, answering the phone when your mother calls, etc.

But when you do, it will be just awful. Gwen will first make it very clear that you have utterly broken up her routine. That her life lives and dies on said routine and that the whole crux of her despair lies in the fact that she does not get enough sleep. For really she would be happy if we would just not call her when she was about to get ready for bed, or rather when she was right in the middle of a continuum that ultimately would lead her to going to bed. For instance: one time I called, and she told me that she was (amid frequent sighs) finally catching up on her hand-lettering exercises and that all she needed to be happy in her miserable, exhausting life would be to finally get caught up on her calligraphy studies. I tried to say something like, "Well, do you want me to go? I mean, I can call another time?" for which she sighed heavily and said, "No."

But let us move along. So, Gwen called you and has left an irresistible message that inferred the actual possibility that she loves and needs you and that you might be the one to save her. Next, you pick up the phone and call her on a Tuesday night around eight in the evening. She pretty quickly makes you feel like a total jackass for calling but nonetheless continues to propel the conversation forward. Just understand that Gwen has her ways to tell you things about herself and her life that will also include ways to tell you that you really should be suspicious regarding your sense of being a pretty good person. She likes to date a lot. She has a terrible and fascinating family. She will never think anything you say is all that good. She will never tell you that you are handsome or funny or talented. She will put just about all of your opinions down as stupid (but note she will not ever say "stupid" but she will infer it by saying "hum" a lot).

Gwen has very open taste regarding both the opposite and same sex when it comes to dating. She will try most everyone once or twice or sometimes over the course of several months without ever really being convinced they deserve her or that they care for her—indeed she swings both ways not only regarding gender but also power—sometimes she loves them more and sometimes they love her more. And they will be interesting. They will be super interesting, so much so, that you will find yourself as addicted to her love life as she is in forging one. One gentleman had a strange condition that his penis did not engorge properly. It stayed thin and limp at the base and rod with a big, hard swinging ball at the end. He also was fleeing his fundamental Christian family from Effingham, IL and was recently diagnosed as being bi-polar. The relationship lasted for around three months, but Gwen found that he was too needy. It took me around twenty minutes to tell my friends about Gwen's boyfriend from Effingham, IL, because I could not get myself to stop laughing. We spent the rest of the night taking turns swinging around a sock I had stuffed with an orange.

Her relationships were not always that fun, however, and sometimes I really would find myself worrying about her. One time, she had an extremely possessive and violent-tempered girlfriend who always channeled her jealousy by putting Gwen continuously down. I really did worry for her and even created a new rule regarding the telephone, Gwen, and myself. If she called and then hung up and then called immediately again, I promised her that I would pick up no matter what. She balked at this and told me that I was dumb to come up with such an idea and that she would never do something like that. Well, she did, and when I did try to fight through several margaritas to be a good, emergency friend, she was light and calm and was just hanging out at home (it was Saturday night around eleven forty-five) and wanted to talk. So, mind you, if you do find yourself really worried for Gwen and form a rule in like kind, understand that she will say that it is a dumb rule and then use it for her own devices. It is like buying a nice sweater for a friend, and your friend holds up the sweater and says, "Oh thank you, I've been meaning to get something to mop my floors."

Now, after you have called Gwen several times over the span of several months, you will find yourself asking, "Why do I keep calling her?" (If you are a sane and reasonable person.) Indeed, several times over the years of calling Gwen, I have told myself never again. In fact, there was nearly a year I managed to keep from calling her, and in doing so, she matched my revenge and also kept from calling me. At first, it was very difficult. I found myself missing her greatly and realized that through the phone, we had forged a genuine, unique bond. However, the unexpected happened. Gwen called me at a normal time. She called me on a Tuesday night at nine. I was stunned—my heart was even pounding. I almost felt the shy excitement of when a new girl gathers the nerve to call me, and we unlock little autobiographical conversations, and I ruin with doodles or pen stabs whatever it is that is sitting in front of me (my only cookbook is totally destroyed from talking to girls on the phone) (which is not good as it was a housewarming gift from my somewhat mean sister). Gwen was happy. She was single and was working on "doing me." Gwen's mother was coming to town, and that made Gwen upset and happy and then upset, as their relationship was riddled with awesomely unhealthy boundaries. They once both dated a pair of brothers. Not once did Gwen ask anything about me or my life. I did manage to slide in a few updates like my new job and that my sister had a baby and how being an uncle was weird and cool. Her answer was always "hum..." which made my chest squeeze painfully every time she did.

At first, I really did miss talking to Gwen and our funny little phone relationship. It had not been since high school that we actually knew each other as proper in-person people. Not once in the ten years of us being away from our hometown had we managed actually to see each other in person. Of course, we had spoken of perhaps making a plan to see each other, but nothing ever really did materialize. The funny thing was that while we have spoken to each other nearly weekly and definitely monthly since high school graduation, we really were never friends in high school. She had called me, because she was thinking about going to the college I was attending and had called me to ask me what it was like to go there. She got my number from our school directory which also listed what college you were attending. That first night was our most amazing conversation. We talked for hours about everything. I was homesick and just starting school away from home. She told me about having holes in her underwear and being lazy about shaving her legs. She told me her mom was a bitch and that she regretted not going to college right after high school and that community college and living at home sucked. She talked about her girlfriend and that she was feeling bad, because she was having thoughts about boys. I talked about music and my favorite book *The River Why* by David James Duncan.

Then, after a few months of being Gwen phone call free, I came to feel something else. I came to feel a new kind of freedom and lightness, and I realized that Gwen was pretty messed up and that she only talked about herself. I started to feel better about myself. I started to talk to other girls on the phone and actually began to ask more girls out—realizing that Gwen had been filling a kind of girl-tank inside of me. But Gwen was terrible fuel.

So, when Gwen did finally walk across that burning bridge and call me on a reasonable night at a reasonable time, I was, at first, excited. I was shocked too, because never in a million years would I expect her to call at nine at night on a Tuesday evening. However, as the adrenaline and initial happiness of being remembered and considered by Gwen wore off, it became more noticeable than ever how she never let me speak, never complimented me or built me up in any way (even though I had been a veritable marching band over the years for her ever-crumbling self-esteem). When I did finally manage to squeeze in a sentence or two regarding my life, all she would say was this somewhat condescending, "Hum...."

The telephone call had whizzed past an hour, and once again, my heart was pounding. Only this time, it was not because I was surprised and excited. This time, my heart was racing, because I was growing extremely angry as Gwen's complaining went on and on, and as every suggestion I offered like, "Why don't you make a point not to spend your quarters when you get change, and so you will always have some for the meter? That's what I do," her response was that she rarely used cash, and besides it seemed stupid to keep track of coins. Then she went on and on regarding the pestilence that coins were, and somehow, she made it seem personal that people were giving her such cumbersome things and that she really could not understand any fool that uses quarters.

Then finally mid-sentence of her nearly crying, because nickels are so *icky and smooth*, I sighed loudly and shouted, "Gwen!"

She then kept on talking. By now, she had jumped from coins to the horrible cost of her books for school and that it was not fair and that if she were running a college, she would offer the books for free. My heart was now really pounding. So much so, I was actually having chest pains. My hands were sweating. "Gwen!" I shouted again.

And again, she just kept on talking. On and on she went. Now she was telling me about how she was seeing a boy with a glass eye and that everything was well and good excepting that she kept having nightmares about the missing eye. By now my mouth was dry, and I was slipping from anger to fear. I was a good guy. I never yelled at girls. I had never hung up on anyone. "Gwen!" I yelled, but this time, it was a full-on scream. It was the loudest scream I had ever made. It was intense. It made me feel awful inside. I felt like a monster.

Gwen's response was total silence. Total complete horrifying silence. In a few seconds, I could hear a sniffle, and it was clear she was beginning to cry.

"I am so sorry. I am so sorry, Gwen. Really, oh my god, I am sooo sorry," I said as softly as I could.

Gwen blew her nose. "That's okay," she said softly. "Everyone has their bad days...." She trailed off with a lilt. "I should probably go now."

"Gwen, don't be like that. We can't just end things like this," I said, feeling horrible and already cooling down.

"No, seriously, it's been well over an hour. I need to go."

I said okay, and we both said goodbye more than once and told each other to take care and have a great evening. And never before did I feel so odd or conflicted. I almost had broken free, and yet now because of my outburst, we were most likely bound forever in this hellish phone relationship.

With that said, I have to say that Phone Call Gwen is really, really one of my most terrible of terrible girls.

The Fishpond
(Marianne)

The goldfish pond was about the size of an inflatable wading pool. The water was mud-colored, yet the orange fish could be seen wagging and darting. Large abalone shells encircled the pond. Some of them had green pools of water and grains of dirt and malachite in them; some of them were dry and shining. The silvery cups, the see-through mud-water, the orange feathery fish, and the surrounding garden was a singular image of perfect beauty for three-year-old Randel. Randel found that if he stood absolutely still and looked at the pond—but did not focus his eyes sharply on the pond—he could take in the complete picture.

The garden was quiet. His great aunt and mother were sitting inside. They were sitting inside next to a large plate-glass window that looked out onto the garden. It was warm and gray outside. He could see them perfectly—there was no glare from the sun. The glass just seemed to tint the women slightly green.

A cricket started to chirp. Randel looked around for it. No cricket could be found. It seemed to Randel that a cricket was solely a song. He had tracked crickets before, but never, no matter how loud and clear the song, did he find one.

Now he could hear one again.

Randel crouched down low. The cricket was close. This was the closest he had ever felt to a cricket. The chirp continued to lazily slide and rattle as Randel stooped over the abalone shells.

"Nooo!" yelled his mother. The screen door slammed loudly shut.

Randel, startled by his mother, lost his balance. He went plunging into the pond. The water was tepid, surprisingly tasteless, and smelled like potting soil. (Randel knew potting soil; it had a grit he could feel in his ears when he ate it.)

"Randel! Bad boy...you could've drowned," said his mother, Marianne, as she swooped him out of the pond.

Randel, still in shock, watched his great aunt hustle towards them with a large white towel. The water between him and his mother was already warm.

"Hand'em to me, Marianne," said Randel's Great Aunt Anna.

Randel's mother handed him to Auntie Anna.

Auntie Anna wrapped him snugly in the towel and hugged him. "My little wet booger," she cooed.

"Booger is right," said Marianne as she shook her head side to side.

"Let's get you stripped, so I can put your clothes in the dryer...you too Marianne...your dress is soaked," said Auntie Anna.

Marianne looked down at her thin cotton dress. The fabric was printed to look like a patchwork of denim and bandanas. The whole front of her dress was dark and plastered to her thin body.

The three sat in the kitchen eating home-preserved peaches and ice-cream as they waited for their clothes to dry. Marianne was wearing a short-sleeved, seersucker housecoat and Randel was wearing an enormous pair of women's underwear held up with a clothespin cinching his waist. They were white and made of nylon. Randel kept sliding on his chair.

The dryer buzzer sounded. Auntie Anna disappeared and reappeared with their clothes. Marianne left with her dress.

"Come here, Randy," said his great aunt. Auntie Anna dressed Randel in the kitchen.

His clothes smelled wonderful; they smelled like Auntie Anna.

Auntie Anna, after dressing him, hugged him and kissed him and carried him back out into the garden.

"This garden is magical, you know," she said.

"Magic?" asked Randel.

"Indeed," answered Auntie Anna as she put the three-year-old down. "Now be a good boy, Randel, and stay away from the fishpond...okay?" asked his great aunt.

Randel shook his head and darted out to a circular patch of fresh herbs.

The sun had turned bright and hot. The plate-glass windows of the house were now enormous mirrors. Randel could see a thin strip of the pond in the windows. Randel tried to stare into the reflection of the pond the same way he had stared into the pond, but the effect was not the same. The reflection of the pond did not marry the garden and the summer air the way the pond did. Randel, however, was a smart boy; he did not want to be charged by a frantic parent again; he decided on a different sensory pleasure. Randel knelt down next to the herbs and began taste-testing all the fragrant plants before him. Sage sort of tasted like Band-Aids. Thyme was bitter. Mint tasted like chewing gum, and parsley made his tongue tingle. Randel decided to put them all in his mouth at once. He realized that if he sat still and just stared off into the plate-glass windows, all the herbs in his mouth formed a singular flavor. Randel smiled gleefully. Tooth-chopped herbs and saliva dripped down his chin. It was a perfect flavor.

Sex

Harry Dunbar's One Night Affair (Agnes)

Pleasure is complicated.

Such a little sentence, yet when Harry Dunbar entered The Opium Room at The East St. Clare Hotel, it sounded as if God himself had whispered it. Harry was supposed to meet up with a few of his friends across the town at a popular restaurant named The Tower; however, on his way, he felt an unusual choking feeling and asked his driver to pull over and let him out at The East St. Clare Hotel.

"Pleasure is complicated," she said with slight Latina accent as the bartender served her another vodka on the rocks.

"It is," said Harry Dunbar as he saddled up charmingly distant from her. There was not quite a full seat's worth of room between them. However, it was clear he had pulled his barstool just slightly farther from the woman than barstools are ordinarily placed. The effect made him seem just a little larger than normal and caused both parties to lean in a little more than normal to speak.

"You smell just like the American Dream," she said while holding up her drink to him.

Harry's throat slacked, and his chest grew into a wide smile. He then laughed. "I sure hope not," he answered while simultaneously ordering a beer.

"How old are you?" she asked.

"Twenty-five," answered Harry Dunbar, now completely turned towards her.

"That is quite an age," she answered. The woman then leaned towards Harry Dunbar, "Tell me, American Dream, for you, is it salt or steel?

"You are a very naughty girl," said Harry. "And very beautiful." He added with a gulp of beer and absolute sincerity. For, in truth, the woman was absolutely beautiful. It was clear to Harry Dunbar who and what she was, and it was very clear to the woman that Harry knew who and what she was. And while she was in her late sixties, years of disciplined grooming and professionalism had forged a permanent grace like that of an ancient shrine (for which age and wear only enhances its proof of potency). "My name is Harry Dunbar," said Harry while offering his hand.

"Agnes Vargas," she replied. "Well, which is it?" she asked. "Salt or steel?"

Harry took a deep, exotic breath. "Salt," he answered.

"I am so relieved," she answered. "Men of steel will break your heart, but men of salt tickle it. Sadly for me, I retired on a man of steel." The woman then put her hand on Harry's leg (for which Harry felt a surprise light strike of heat underneath her simple, warm gesture).

Harry had on many occasions been with a courtesan, though never yet at his unmarried age had he been with a concubine—the lesser but beloved *other wife*—the Hagar. He had seen them, of course, and even assumed that when he became heavy with wife and children that he too would find and take one. His father, of course, had more than one and even had been almost taken over by one had it not been for the death of Harry's baby brother. Harry wondered if his father would have really divorced his mother and ran off with what he claimed to be *the love of his life*. However, after his baby brother died, his father simply limped away from the family (leaving his marriage intact) to live a strange life of drinking and painting in Montana with absolutely no heart for love, salt, or steel. Only once did Harry Dunbar visit Sr. Dunbar as a recluse artist, and it would become what Harry would privately consider as *the worst mistake of his life*.

"Ah, matters of the heart," began Harry, "I have no real idea where I stand with my heart. I am surrounded by girls I am not so sure about. They are lovely to look at though."

"How very ingenious of you. I mean, how else is a man to find himself if he cannot sort out all the women around him?"

"Oh, my dear lovely Agnes," said Harry Dunbar. "You're smart."

"Be careful with me," said Agnes in a soft trailing voice.

"I'll take a double scotch," said a startlingly familiar voice next to Harry.

"Phil?" asked Harry, looking up.

"Harry," returned Phil Popper. Phil then took his drink down in one gulp. "Thank god you are here, or maybe my problems will be worsened...I am in way over my head tonight, old friend."

"What is the matter?" asked Harry laughing (though his heart was also sinking, for Phil's presence had immediately broken his spell with Agnes Vargas).

"Do you promise not to punch me? You see, I have sort of found myself on a date with a girl I know you call on regularly—though in all honesty it really all happened accidentally," answered Phil with very white ringed eyes.

"I am quite sure, Phil, that I am not going to punch you," returned Harry Dunbar with a very subtle tone of annoyance.

"Well, you see, I was supposed to go out with Ashley Lemmings, but when I called to verify our date, she told me that she had invited Charlie Tipple to join us. Which to be honest sort of deflated me, as it seemed to me a clear signal that Ashley wanted to dilute any potential romantic energies that might have arisen over dinner. Anyway, when I went to pick up Ashley, she and Charlie came to the door, only Ashley was in her bathrobe and Charlie was in a very tight black leather motorcycle jacket. I was so confused by their outfits that I momentarily froze into one of the most awkward greetings ever. I had not only offered one hand out to shake with Ashley but another out towards Charlie. So there I was in their little foyer standing in front of them frozen in the position of a kind of coarse, mid-stride robot pose with both hands extended to shake hopelessly in mid-air." Phil then motioned for another drink, requesting the next one to be a single. "Anyway, neither Ashley nor Charlie shook my offering hands...though I hardly blame them, as it was not very clear that was my intention. Instead, the two girls gave each other a little kiss, and Charlie was leading me out to what I was brusquely informed as her *brand-new baby*. Now stop laughing Harry, because this is serious. I really can't believe I am here now able to speak to you, and really there is still every possibility that tonight will be my last supper, and to make matters worse, the head chef is off away on some vacation, and I have a very pouty Charlie Tipple on my hands picking through her very unexciting but normally terribly exciting *St. Clare Caesar* and no doubt plotting how she can take me back to my car in the most reckless way possible on her new motorcycle...for which when I did ask if she had a motorcycle license she only laughed and told me not to be such a *dickhead*." Phil paused to gather himself. "And that isn't even the scariest part. I fear that somehow someway I am going to say something or do something that is going to tick her off, and there is a great possibility I will. I'm just no good under pressure, Oh Harry, what am I going to do?"

"Phil, calm down," calmly said Harry. "Charlie is really not so bad. You just need to know how to deal with her. First off, have you told her that she is around a thousand times lovelier than not only Abby Turner but also Maxie Mansard?"

"No, but to be honest, I spent the first part of our date trying to not die on the back of her motorcycle," returned Phil, who had already written down Harry's first tip on a small leather bound notebook.

"Telling Charlie Tipple that she is lovely will only anger her...Charlie needs to be called *lovelier*, not simply lovely. Next, you then need to tell her that some part of her face or body is terribly unattractive. I have lately been picking on her nose, so you might want to throw a little weight in that direction, as it will have an even greater sedative effect on her. Finally, after dinner, which will be short, as she does not ever eat past the starter menu, you need to take her back to a fine, but not too fine, hotel and screw her as if your whole life depended on it, for really old chap, if you don't, she really might find a way to eject you from her new motorcycle."

"I think I just threw up in my mouth," sighed Phil Popper with very jittery eyes. "I better go." Phil then gently—almost intently gently—set his empty glass on the bar and somberly walked out of The

Opium Room.

"I'm sorry about that," said Harry Dunbar as he turned towards Agnes Vargas. And then for a brief, foreign moment, Harry Dunbar felt a surge of regret. She was no longer there. She had left. He had not even noticed or acknowledged her leaving, and with that thought, an even greater pang of regret arose, for surely only the very finest of concubines could slink so deftly away. "Barkeep?" hailed Harry, "Does the woman who was sitting next to me frequent this place often?"

"I never speak of good women," answered the bartender.

"You're a good man," returned Harry. Harry then left the bartender a large tip and gathered himself to go. His heart was leaden, and the choking sensation had returned—only not nearly as gripping as it had been before. As he walked through the lobby, he pulled out his phone and a cigarette and wondered if his old plans and old friends were still at The Tower while also wondering if he really could go across town and be *Harry Dunbar* with them. As Harry was exiting the hotel while lighting his cigarette, he slammed right into a fur-wrapped Agnes. It appeared that she had not fully departed—she had only stepped out for a cigarette and was utterly pleased that her American Dream had run into her.

Once again in her drawing presence, Harry thought of his two-year-old brother passing away at the hospital from leukemia and his booze-broken father sweating away in his isolated ranch studio before Agnes asked him who his silly friend was. "Phil Popper," answered Harry Dunbar, who was now standing so close to her he could look down at the top of her head.

"What does Phil Popper do? He looks like a man who does something," asked Agnes.

"He is a translator of poetry," answered Harry Dunbar.

"Oh, so we are in the same business," she returned.

"Listen, Agnes, do you want to go someplace?" asked Harry with a slightly raised and broken tone. The tonal break with his voice was very subtle, though still poignant enough to slightly sting both of their egos.

Agnes drew in a very deep breath of the chilly, late February air. She knew he was both curious and drawn to her but also scared of her age. Agnes knew this bodily fear all too well, as it was she fifty years ago who felt it when she went upstairs with her first old man. And much like Harry Dunbar, she too had felt an awkward mix of curiosity and attraction as well as fear and repulsion of what one would find in touching a human so old. "I am not sure that is what you want, my dear American Dream," she answered cautiously.

Harry did not answer quickly after, and this pause left Agnes with yet another insight. While it did indeed pinch her ego a great deal to be offered such a gingerly pass, it had nonetheless made her heart riot in a way that felt as true as it ever had at any other point in her life. "The heart does not age," thought Agnes. This heart riot, however, was cruel, as she knew that if it were to go unappeased, surely the pain would be greater than the inner dormancy had been before Harry's suggestion. With terror, Agnes spoke, "I have a suite upstairs if you would like to come in from the cold."

Harry Dunbar bent his lips so close to her ear as to almost graze it. "Lead the way," he said without the slightest trace of youth-bearing hesitation.

The journey to her suite felt just like deep warm drugs to Harry Dunbar. The fine wood paneled elevator pulsed like a gently swaying mink coat; the lights down the hallway glowed like softly singing snowballs. She walked ahead of him with her long fur coat and dark hair swaying. Her hair was set in large, tipsy curls, and the pin-prick of her heels disappeared into the plush red carpet; her smell was the most decent scent Harry had ever remembered following, and he truly wondered if it was her or perfume. If Agnes had known that Harry had wondered whether or not her perfect scent was her or her perfume, it would have meant the world to her. If Harry had known that his thoughts regarding her scent would have meant so much to her, he would have uncharacteristically told her. Instead, she simply opened the door to her suite, and he followed her in, sitting immediately on the bed, and taking off his top coat.

"What would you like to drink? I do have

everything," cleanly offered Agnes.

"What are you having?" returned Harry Dunbar.

"Champagne," answered Agnes Vargas. "But come here." Agnes motioned Harry to join her at the large floor to ceiling windows. She then handed him a glass of wine. "This is where we are. This is what The East St. Clare sees," she said. "Every time I look out into the city at night, I always like to make a point to locate really, absolutely where I am. Otherwise, one can get terribly lost."

Harry wanted to say, *If you keep talking to me that way I am going to come apart*, but luckily, Agnes really was terribly good at being what she was. After gently toasting the city, she set her glass down and disappeared into another room in the suite.

In front of the chilly, tall window of The East St. Clare, Harry took off his suit coat and tie. He then unbuttoned his shirt down to the middle of his chest, revealing a crisp new undershirt and a small gold cross that his brother had worn as he struggled with leukemia in the hospital. The cross was so very tiny, so little, made for a baby. When his mother gave it to him after his brother's funeral, Harry thought that such a little thing should only be put in a box, but as Harry grew into adulthood, he increasingly saw its worth as a precious amulet. At first, he wore it before big soccer games that he wanted to win at boarding school and later during exams at college. Since graduation into the free-floating world of his adult life, he found it nearly impossible not to see its need; he wore it now nearly always. His whole life had blurred into a soccer game and final exam, and yet there was nowhere he had to go; this rough clash of hurried worry to win and of no game or challenge or real-world check had recently begun to invade Harry Dunbar's senses. Sometimes he felt like he was choking, and sometimes he felt as though he could not feel anything at all. His cross was a great issue as he took off his clothes, because he had a kind of policy or rule concerning his brother's cross and that was it was never to be seen by another and certainly not while Harry was engaging in being Harry. Harry had nearly no rules, so actually having one at least served to form a faint outline between himself and the vast, drizzly city.

Agnes stood before the broad, well-lit bathroom mirror trembling. Never did she think she would be in this position again at her age and certainly not with the American Dream. Harry was not only exceedingly wealthy and well mannered, but he was also impossibly handsome. There was some humor though in her plight, as she knew Harry would have been her undoing if she would have met him when she was young. She would not have been able to keep or hold on to the truth of her place, and only misery would have come to her if she would have fallen in love and forgotten who and what she actually was.

Agnes indeed had not been, however, wholly celibate in her newly entered winter, and she knew how to prepare for a delicate union of age, pleasure, and concealment. She massaged her whole body with lotion so that touch would still be good, and she wore a long, red satin nightgown with a matching, floor-length robe. The long sleeves and tightly cinched waist of the robe were skin snug and girdled her thin, still handsome form. Her breasts were always very small and still took mouths and rubbing hands well. Her hair, on all regions, was still soft, undyed dark brown with only the barest tinseling of silver. Her Honduran heritage had blessed her with a hearty, natural beauty. In short, her eyes were never *ever* going away. Harry Dunbar had espied that bare fact immediately upon meeting her, and if he had only told her, perhaps. But he did leave his cross on when he crawled into bed, and that little fact heralded not only a broken rule—an erasing—but also a tripped line. Harry was taking a risk for her—something he never really did for anyone—especially himself.

Harry Dunbar was surprised and charmed by the fact that Agnes Vargas did not dim or turn off the lights before she came to him, for even the girls his age often did that. Indeed, it was playful and funny and a little noisy, for she brought the champagne over with glasses to the bedside, but the smoke from the cigarette in her mouth momentarily impaired her vision, and in trying to still herself she spilled the wine and dropped one of the glasses. Harry jumped out of bed quickly to assist her, and she laughed and sang something in Spanish. He was completely naked and already had a hard-on which seemed to make her sing in Spanish. Harry became uncharacteristically shy with his excitement revealed, and for that funny little moment, both could easily be referred to as *kids*.

Harry returned to the bed and began to crawl in. Agnes gently told him not to. She then knelt on the bed next to him and gently touched his torso and lower regions. She took a last drink of wine. Her soft, fragrant hair dragged over his face and chest, and life began to suspend for Harry Dunbar. Her hair then dragged over his legs and slowly, like a warm, mythical snake, she wound up his trunk. All points awakened, but not in an electrical way, rather in an unfurling way. She was opening up every nerve in his body like the opening up of a flower. The sensation was almost unbearably pleasurable. Concubines are different and unique in skills than wives or courtesans, and no more did this become abundantly clear to Harry when, out of reckless need, he climbed on top of her and went into her, whereupon she transformed instantly into a magic raft made of red satin and every dream of man. And with each stroke, he felt as though he could finally plunge into that place—that place that all of his orgasms had stopped short—had somehow evaded. The deeper and harder he pressed into her, the snugger and more potent she felt. They were way beyond The East St. Clare Hotel, the city, the bed, their forms—they were rowing away. She had not made him simply stand on the shore and enjoy the sea as all girls had in the past; she had outright melted him all the way down. Harry Dunbar and Agnes Vargas finally managed to row away that night. "There really is *the other side*," thought Harry as Agnes finally fell away from him.

"Tell me something about yourself," she said as she handed him a glass of wine.

Harry propped up his pillows and leaned up against the padded headboard. "I am not a very good person," he returned.

Agnes laughed. "That is a good thing to know early," she replied.

"How about you?" asked Harry, "Tell me something now."

"My father was a violinist. He was actually quite good. We traveled together all over the world, and I think he might have been great if I was a better wife to him. But you know, I was not even a good daughter to him," she answered.

"Where was your mother?" asked Harry.

"She died when I was young," said Agnes. "But now it is your turn in this game. Tell me something else."

"Let's see," began Harry, "I have three sisters, and I think all of them are absolutely terrible. The youngest is still in college and seems to do nothing but cry. The other two are older than me and are hard and unhappy."

Agnes let out a small laugh. "Are they married?" she asked with a little bit of embarrassment in her voice from having laughed.

"The eldest and the next eldest are engaged. The little one has a boyfriend," he answered.

"They must all look like you. Are they all

terribly lovely?" she asked.

"It's my turn. Tell me something more," said Harry, wanting out of the topic.

"I am terribly fond of tennis, and for most of my life, I have tried to play every day," she answered.

"Really?" asked Harry.

"Do not be so surprised...just because we met in The Opium Room does not mean I do not survive the light of day," she gently scolded.

"I love tennis too," quietly said Harry with just the faintest of yawns, "Excuse me."

"Let us go to sleep," said Agnes, who then leaned deeply over Harry and turned out his bedside lamp before turning off her own.

Agnes was gone in the morning, but orange juice, a scone, and a note were left for him. She was off to play tennis. She was very happy they had met. She thought he was a very good bad man. *Such a night, love Agnes.* He folded the card and put it in the inside pocket of his suit coat. "She really did play tennis and really could survive the light," thought Harry.

Harry strolled through the mid-sized, though incredibly handsome, hotel lobby feeling perfectly lucky. He was in love but not in a way that took any of his sense of being and good and bad away. There was absolutely nothing that he needed to get rid of to love Agnes Vargas. All he would have to do is spoil her; it was a perfect thing. All he would have to do was pay for her life; it was such a completely perfect thing.

"Harry? Harry, is that you?" asked an exceedingly familiar voice.

"Phil?" asked Harry extremely annoyed to have been discovered in such a romantic state. Quickly and hauntingly, Harry completely dropped Agnes Vargas from his mind. "So, did you roger old Charlie?" asked Harry Dunbar jovially.

"I am not sure what I really did with Charlie Tipple. She is a very strong girl," answered Phil Popper with a great deal of worry in his voice. "In fact, through a great deal of our love making, she spoke of her personal trainer and all of the special projects they were working on regarding her thighs, arms, and, I believe, feet...which I suspect could not be right...but somehow my memory is clinging to the idea. I did, however, manage to triumph momentarily during a bit of a land grab...I managed to get one of her breasts steadily in my mouth for a while without being completely routed by a bone crushing thigh grip. All in all, as I am not limping anymore, I am going to call it a moderate success...I mean I have had worse...a lot worse. She does talk a lot during sex though, which is unnerving only because I kept losing my focus...not only did I learn a great deal about what it takes to be Charlie Tipple's body, but I also learned a great deal of interesting girl gossip. It turns out Maxie Mansard's little Lily...her little pet acolyte...is causing quite a stir at college, declaring that as long as it stops at heavy petting, she can date as many boys as she would like and that it still would not make her a slut...of course, the whole timber of Charlie's story regarding little, fair Lily was definitely leaning towards mockery and the general dubiousness of such a declaration. You now know my whole night, old friend...please inform yours truly as to why it is you are up so early and why you are in the lobby of The East St. Clare?" returned Phil Popper.

"I spent the evening with a most delightful prostitute," answered Harry Dunbar.

The two gentlemen exited the hotel to a bright, freezing morning. Harry's eyes and constitution greatly squinted, as he was wholly unaccustomed to the city's morning rush hour.

"Are all these people going to work?" asked Harry.

"Harry, I pray for your sake that nothing in this world ever changes," laughed Phil, "I just can't see you doing anything...and yet the funny thing about you is that everything you do is always perfect...I always feel so guilty when I find myself jealous of you...I mean no one should ever want to be you."

"Thanks, old chap," returned Harry as he lit a cigarette.

"See what I mean? Nobody...absolutely nobody takes criticism as well as you...looks like you are going to be the star once again at my analyst's appointment today...well you and oh god here she comes...." Phil Popper began to turn pale green.

Charlie Tipple pulled up to the hotel's entrance on her motorcycle. She was wearing high heels, a very skintight mini-dress, and a skintight motorcycle jacket. She was not wearing any underwear, and both Harry, Phil, and most likely a good portion of the oncoming traffic were treated to her great divide. "It looks like your new girl has come to retrieve you," said Harry Dunbar with a low, perfected, evil voice.

"It is not as bad as it looks...she is not, well... we lost her underwear in the restaurant. She had taken them off in an effort to flirt with me and liven up the rather boring cuisine. She had handed them to me at the same time the busboy was coming to take our plates, and somehow her underwear got caught up in the transaction. We did, however, have a rather intent and doting water service for the rest of the night, so it was not a complete loss," retorted Phil Popper.

"It looks like the therapy is working...you really are clinging to the sunny side of life," said Harry laughing.

"Enough with the chatter, girls...Phil, come on! I have to be at the gym in less than an hour!" yelled Charlie Tipple over the loud engine of her bike.

"Good luck!" yelled Harry as he watched them speed away.

Harry happily dragged off his cigarette as he swung himself loosely through the pressing, intent crowds. It was safe again to think of Agnes Vargas. Harry thought of her and their night and felt as though finally he was going to get away with something that actually meant something. He was going to, at least for a little while, have a little of this love that everybody around him seemed to moan about; love was something Harry never felt for anyone. Now, he was going to have a little bit of love, and he would not have to do much for it. This was something he never seriously thought he would or could achieve, and yet, here it was.

"The first thing I am going to do is buy her a present," thought Harry to himself. "What a delight this love is...what wonderful little chores...today I will find the perfect present for Agnes Vargas." And a very delighted Harry drifted through the city with something to do.

* * *

"So, Abby, what is it that you are working on now?" asked Harry Dunbar.

Abby Turner was a funny friend for Harry Dunbar. She was his exception. He had known her since boarding school. Abby was nothing like anyone else in Harry's life, and every time he thought of her, his neck stiffened. He did not like her gentleness or kindness, and he especially disliked her vulnerability. She always seemed to him as a kitten stuck high in a tree. He hated this almost continuous inability in her, because he always found himself worrying about her. She was very beautiful. However, her loveliness only irritated him more, as it was the worst kind of loveliness a girl could possess, as he knew he would have no idea what to do with her if he were to ever catch her. Her beauty almost seemed more like a natural defense rather than a drawer of danger like most women's beauty. Even in her most horrible moments, when Harry was moved to finally shout her down and show her all of her terrible ways, he found her beauty to check him at the start. He would then be reduced to bribing her with a promise of a zoo visit if only she would stop talking and see his point of view. But here he was, once again, over at her queer apartment carved out of an enormous mansion in the city she had inherited from her grandparents. She had turned the great house's ballroom into her living quarters. Harry both loved it there and hated it there; it was such a strange place; it was a home built by a kitten stuck high in a tree with absolutely no idea how to get down.

"I am currently taking a Peruvian cuisine cooking class," answered Abby. "It is difficult—nearly as difficult as it was studying Ikebana, Japanese flower arranging. I got yelled at a great deal in that class. I think it was way too Zen for me or that I was not Zen enough for Ikebana."

"So besides Peruvian cooking, what else have you been up to?" asked Harry.

"You are sure asking me a lot of questions this evening...what is going on, Harry? You hate asking people what it is they are up to. And surely, my life would be the very last life you would want to be informed of. I see your face sour when I open up conversations with what book it is I am currently reading," returned Abby.

And that was it; that was the magnetism and the repellent of Abby Turner. She expressed exactly what she saw, and more often than not, she was able to see the truth. What she was terrible at, and why Harry never felt safe around her, was that she had very little ability to hold back her observations. What kept Harry from outright hating her was that she had a naïve kindness and genuine oafishness that tempered much, if not all, of what she said. "I had a very strange week, and I believe I became a little more lost than usual," answered Harry.

Abby laughed warmly. "Impossible," she said.

"What do you mean *impossible*?" asked Harry.

"First of all, Harry, you are never lost. Sure, you like to open every single door you encounter, but you always simply look in...you never fully enter any of those doors," she answered.

Harry took in an involuntary deep breath as he stood up. "I am going to the kitchen to make some margaritas," said Harry as he made his way to the kitchen. Harry firmly planted both of his hands on the kitchen counter before he moved to make the cocktails. He needed to be alone for a moment. He needed to be away from Abby for just a second to rebuild his walls. She was very right, and she was very wrong. "I did walk through Agnes' door," thought Harry to himself. "Abby is wrong. I did walk through Agnes' door...." And then Harry's heart sank. "But did I? Damn it...did I or did I not walk through Agnes' door?" Harry began to reflexively make margaritas as he pondered Agnes and whether or not he had indeed walked through her door. There was great cause for question, as although Harry Dunbar did purchase Agnes Vargas a very fine present the day after their night, he had not yet delivered it. He was all set the very next night, but as he was having a few pre-Agnes cocktails at The Tower, an old friend from college had arrived with two hippie girls in tow. His old friend had a rather ornate story of spiritual awakening via psychedelic drugs and tantric sex down in Mexico, and when it was revealed that the two girls in tow were indeed highly recommended practitioners of sex magic, and when it was revealed that his friend had his father's penthouse for the week along with enough drugs to not have to touch earth anytime soon, well, the gift slept forgotten in his topcoat for a week. Agnes too was dormant. Well, not totally.

For the most part, the *practitioners* Harry's friend so heavily lauded were small-lived girls living in a broad landscape. Their sense of "sex magic" seemed to Harry like so many other human magics in that it was a mysticism born out of vulnerability—something Harry detested in others. He hated seeing people with coughs or bandages. The girls would light incense and chant before mounting him and his friend. On more than one occasion, Harry found himself torn between the natural want of sex and repulsion as the girls would roll their heads back and shout to the goddess while mounted on top of him or wriggling beneath him. And always this shouting, humping, incense, and chanting was meant to produce something they wanted. To the goddess we pray for and to the goddess we ask for and to the goddess we need to bring in our lives: gasoline for their van in order to make it to an ashram in upstate New York, tuition for one of the girls to go to massage therapy school, and of course, peace on earth. Somehow a deep and rolling orgasm was supposed to conjure, bring forth the great creation's sense of duty towards man and would somehow bring these deeply desired things to the ladies.

They were generous, however, not only with their bodies, but on more than one occasion, they pressed both Harry Dunbar and his old college friend what it was they wanted from the goddess. Harry's old college friend, while nursing one of the girls and being pleasured via her speaking mouth by the other, was periodically asking the goddess for inner peace and for his father to relent and allow him to continue on his spiritual quest (which of course by *relent* he meant *finance*). Indeed, for a great deal of the time, both girls worked Harry's friend ambitiously, using every possible pliability in an effort for his friend's magical wish to come true, as it seemed to be the one wish that really—truly would solve everyone's problems. For Harry, the drugs were so good that most of the time Harry did not want his trip to be tripped up by a great deal of licking and tugging. Again though, they were generous, and when Harry wanted a bit of an embrace, they had plenty of juice left for him. There were some tensions over that week however, and while most were generated between the two girls and Harry's friend and their lack of future income, Harry refusing to ask the goddess for anything also proved contentious, as one of the girls claimed that it made her feel "used" and "cheap" to simply have sex with Harry, while sex magic, the girls argued, was *holy work*. It also did not help when Harry, while one of the girls was riding on top of him shouted, "He wished the goddess would get the girl on top of him to shut up!" When these eruptions did occur, all was smoothed over as Harry's friend would call the girls over to a discreet corner and explain to them that Harry was their patron for the week and if all went well would leave them a parting gift that would most likely get them to the ashram, which Harry did of course.

But there was one moment in which Agnes Vargas shockingly came to Harry's mind, and it did rattle him greatly and made him feel uncharacteristically unsure about whether or not he was having a good time. Normally, Harry Dunbar glided through liquidy scenes with a kind of Lord of the Manor ownership. Harry always felt an ownership when it came to pleasures of the flesh. However, when Agnes sharply arose in his mind and memory, Harry felt the sharp prick of being a serf. While it was fleeting and easily healed with a mushroom cap and some very good weed (not to mention some of his friend's father's very fine wine), there was enough of a scar to cause him to almost want to tell Abby Turner about it in her ballroom apartment. It was around three in the afternoon, and everyone (so Harry thought) was in a deep sleep in his college friend's dad's penthouse. The sun was low but strangely deep yellow in color, and it delivered just the tiniest morsel of summer to the late winter light. Harry was on his way to the kitchen to get himself a glass of water. He was completely naked—indeed he had been so (barring some protective beads the girls had decorated him with) for the past forty-eight hours. As he entered the kitchen, he espied one of the girls washing some of her panties and bras in the kitchen sink. Harry froze and watched her; she remained completely unaware he was there. She was wearing nothing but an apron leaving her back and bottom completely exposed; her hair was knotted up loosely on top of her head, and a few of the late winter sun rays were streaking the brown locks into a deep reddish gold color. It was the first time that whole week Harry had seen anything beautiful, and he felt deeply relieved. Seeing the young drifter washing her underthings finally gave her some grace and order, making him able to open up his eyes to her. The girl then dropped a pair of her underwear on the floor, and in turning to retrieve it, she leaped back at the sight of Harry. She then turned fully towards Harry with her hand touching her chest as if to signal that she was still under the spell of being frightened and sang out a little song in Spanish. It was the same song Agnes Vargas had sung when she had been surprised by his fully aroused member. Harry took the girl where she stood and tried harder than ever to row away completely with her. He realized, of course, that there are sex magic practitioners, and then there was Agnes Vargas. The sex was good, but at all times he was on the kitchen floor with a young drugged-out drifter in his friend from college's dad's penthouse.

"Are you hiding from me?" gently asked Abby Turner as she entered the kitchen.

"Margaritas are done...now back, back, back away...I am moving out with pitcher and glasses in hand," returned Harry as he walked right towards Abby Turner as a way to corral her and redirect her back to the sitting area of the ballroom.

"Harry," gingerly began Abby, "I can't help but feel that there is something that you want to talk about with me."

"Abby, tell me something," began Harry Dunbar, "you said earlier that you felt that I was someone that was never lost, because I do not enter any of the doors I open. Well, what did you mean by that?"

"I suppose I mean that you always seem, regardless of the situation, to remain Harry...I don't know. I guess I am saying that you do not seem to ever be taken away, affected by anything. I mean, you do all sorts of things...but there always seems to be a kind of field around you." Abby Turner put her drink down and frowned. "At least I think that is what I meant...sometimes I say things, and then when I try to explain the things I had said, I get lost in what it is I meant. I don't know Harry, you just seem very unmovable, but then again, I am entirely feathery, I'm always getting moved all over the place. So, perhaps I need or rather love you to be unmovable. This might be a projection operation at work."

"I hate asking you questions," returned Harry Dunbar.

"I know you do," said Abby Turner, "It is just that I swear I can see something wild behind your skin tonight."

"Do you intend to say the things you say, or is there some deep betrayal on your mouth's part?" asked Harry.

There was then a long pause between the two. Abby sighed and finally spoke, "Well, now you have me afraid to talk, because you might be onto something. I did not want to bring it up, but it seems that lately Maxie and I have been doing nothing but tie our verbal exchanges into terrible little knots, and I end up hanging up the phone or returning home feeling that something bad but very subtly bad had just occurred."

"There is a problematic chemistry between the two of you...to be honest, I do not think this knot situation will ever go away...even if you manage to sync up your mouth with your brain," sighed Harry Dunbar who was growing increasingly anxious to leave.

"What do you mean by that?" asked Abby Turner.

Harry then stood up and stretched. "I have to go now, my little, gorgeous one," he said. Abby rose to walk him out of her mansion. When they made it to the door, Harry took both of Abby Turner's hands lightly. "Abby," he began, "you really are beautiful, and to be honest, I cannot decide if that is a good or bad thing for me."

"You tell me the dumbest things in the world when you want to run from me," returned Abby.

Harry squinted his eyes sharply and feigned disapproval towards Abby Turner. "I have to go," he said.

"Will you ever bother to explain to me why you think Maxie and I will always be in knots?" asked Abby.

Harry broke into a large grin and laughed. "I don't know," he answered. And without any further goodbye, Harry left.

The city was moist and chilly. Spring was near. Harry Dunbar's fingers felt so numb as he walked down the street towards The East St. Clare Hotel that he could barely smoke his cigarette. Other people too seemed jumpy and numb on the streets, as many gently bumped into Harry as he walked, and each time they would laugh, apologize, and swing back into their excited sway. The thought of having a cold beer with Agnes Vargas in The Opium Room made Harry's knees buckle. And one of the first things he was going to do is ask what was that Spanish song she had sung? And one of the first things he was going to say to her was that he was happy to see her and that he missed her. And one of the first things he was going to do when he saw her was give her the little present he had bought for her the morning after their union.

Harry Dunbar absolutely could not feel his body when he entered The East St. Clare Hotel. The air in the hotel was extremely dry and warm and was a striking reminder that winter was still not quite over. The Opium Room was almost empty, as most of the city was running around outside and bumping into each other. Harry sat at the bar and ordered a cold beer. It was a different bartender, and this irritated him greatly. If he had not been so numb with excitement, he most likely would not have been upset by the fact. However, he wanted everything to be just as he had anticipated, and somehow, all of his anticipations also included the original bartender (who had an elderly, somber dignity that the woman somewhere in her middle thirties did not, besides, the woman was wearing the same uniform as the men which was a tuxedo without a jacket—this was something Harry loathed—he hated seeing women dressed as men). However, after a few beers, he softened on his earlier dislike of the female barkeep, and after a few more beers he even began to like the way she spent her lull time polishing bottles and slicing lemons and limes in the most attentive manner Harry had ever seen.

"Listen," began Harry Dunbar as the female bartender handed him his sixth beer, "do you know if a woman named Agnes Vargas has been in here tonight? Or last night for that matter? She is a very lovely woman somewhere in her late sixties? Very dark eyes?"

The woman paused and tilted her head just

slightly to the side. "How do you know her?" she asked.

"We are very dear friends. I actually came here to meet up with her," answered Harry Dunbar.

"You had a planned date?" she asked.

"Well, in a manner of speaking, yes...yes we had a planned date," returned Harry. He lied slightly, fearing that, like the other bartender, this one was also discreet regarding its patrons.

"Excuse me for a minute," she said and then left The Opium Room.

Shortly after, the woman bartender returned with a middle-aged man somewhere in his fifties. He was bald and dressed in a fine gray suit. The bartender returned to polishing bottles as the suited gentleman approached Harry. "Hello," said the gentleman, "my name is John Gerald. I am the manager of The East St. Clare. Mary, our bartender, has informed me that you are a friend of Ms. Agnes Vargas."

"Yes," hesitantly replied Harry Dunbar, fearing that he had entered a kind of trap or trouble involving Agnes Vargas.

"Well, I am not sure how to put this, but your friend," the gentleman paused as if to collect himself (indeed, for he rubbed his forehead). "Last week, your friend was found in her room by one of our cleaning staff. She was sitting in a chair facing out towards the windows. They said the scene seemed almost...almost polite...for what it was...." The man paused again. "I am sorry sir, but your friend committed suicide last week. I wish I could tell you more. It appeared somewhat planned, as quickly some people came from a law office to settle her bill and take possession of her belongings...I am...I am very sorry sir. Please know that anything you've had tonight will most definitely be on us. Again, I am truly sorry...we did not know her well, but she really was a...well, she was a good woman...the staff did comment on how polite and considerate the final scene was...." The man rubbed his forehead again, "I'm sorry I do not mean to be graphic, but we are still, I suppose, upset by the affair...she really was memorable." The man stood and put out his hand out to shake Harry's. Harry gave it to him automatically, and instead of shaking it, the man simply rested his other hand on top of Harry's hand. "Again, I am truly sorry for your loss," he said and then turned and left The Opium Room.

"Do you want another?" softly asked the bartender, Mary, after the manager had left.

"I had better not," answered Harry Dunbar. Harry then slid off his barstool and entered the nearly spring night. Every time people bumped into him, they would laugh and sweetly apologize.

As Harry Dunbar walked the bustling evening streets of the city, he had no idea how he felt about what had just happened. It surely was a surprising event. It was a loss. It was confusing. However, he had loved her in a peculiar way. He loved her but loved her with a caveat that he did not indeed have to change himself in any way to have her.

Consequently, in losing her, he almost felt as though he *ought* to remain unchanged, for really that was the ground of their relationship. But still, there was a kind of silent argument within Harry Dunbar that made the sidewalk beneath his feet rise and fall like a mild, continual earthquake. This silent argument might have genuinely surfaced into a dialogue had not a precious phone call arrived allowing Harry to safely step back onto hard, steady ground.

"Harry, oh thank god you are answering your phone tonight," said a very panicked Phil Popper. "I fear there is going to be a full-scale war within the upper ranks of female society."

"What is going on?" asked Harry.

"Well, Charlie Tipple decided to throw a ladies-only cocktail party, and well, I think Maxie Mansard took it as a kind of power grab for social ranking, and well, things were tense right off the bat. But things have now grown wild, as Charlie and her friends have been increasing their remarks regarding Maxie's most recent young acolyte, Lily, and her virtue. You must come over, as I am the only male here, and I really do not think I am any match for these girls. You know, all these girls are trained in several martial arts—not to mention the fact that they have all been working out since they were in elementary school. I am, dear old friend, completely out of my depth. I recently suggested that we all try to avoid talking about anyone who was not present for which the entire room froze in horror. I was then told to go make more toast points and pomegranate martinis which is what I am doing now," answered Phil Popper.

"Where are you?" calmly asked Harry Dunbar.

"At Charlie Tipple's apartment," returned Phil Popper.

"I will be there shortly," said Harry.

"Thank god. I think I just heard a loud gasp from the other room made by well over three or four girls," returned Phil.

Harry hailed a cab and quickly arrived at Charlie Tipple's building, but before he could exit, he saw his very old (since childhood) friend Maxie Mansard running out of the building. "Maxie!" he yelled from the cab.

Maxie Mansard paused and quickly found Harry Dunbar in her tautly scanning eyes. She then approached the cab. "Phil must have called," she sighed. "Get out of the cab and join me in my car."

Harry Dunbar paid the man and climbed out of the cab. "But what about Phil?" he asked.

"Oh, Phil is way beyond saving," returned Maxie Mansard, "Come, come with me, and I'll fill you in." Maxie Mansard then pulled ahead of Harry with a thoughtfully rushed stride.

Harry paused only briefly—looking up towards Charlie Tipple's apartment—then followed his friend to her waiting car.

"It was just terrible," began Maxie Mansard as she lit a cigarette, "Do we want to go to The Tower? Where are we going?"

"Let's go to The East St. Clare," answered Harry,

completely unaware that his suggestion was telling.

"Oh, I love The Opium Room; I have not been there since I was a child," said Maxie Mansard.

Maxie's car pulled up to the entrance of The East St. Clare. A handsomely uniformed footman opened the car door and told Miss Maxie Mansard, "Good evening." He then jovially touched the rim of his hat to Harry Dunbar.

"This really is a pleasant place," remarked Maxie as the two entered the handsome old hotel. Harry followed his childhood friend into The Opium Room, mildly aware that he was ingesting dark medicine in returning there. However, Maxie Mansard had dignity for flesh and mint for spirit, and she was so utterly pristine that Harry could easily follow Maxie's delicate stomp with very little aftertaste. Harry always felt safe following Maxie around. He had followed her orders since they were children. She was the most polished, strong thing Harry had ever met. He had never seen her cry and always felt safe and peaceful around her knowing that she never would. She was pretty too, very pretty. Her features were all perfectly formed and orderly. Her beauty was of having absolutely nothing wrong. The only little check mark against her in Harry's eyes was just how much Maxie knew she was pretty. Whenever she entered a room, it was almost as if by the way she carried herself and said hello that she was saying, "Yes, I know, I am terribly pretty aren't I?" This was the little stone in his shoe regarding his dear old friend Maxie; somehow in knowing so completely that she was pretty, it made her a little less so. Harry Dunbar ordered them a bottle of champagne and was relieved that the previous female bartender was no longer there. It was now a middle-aged gentleman he had never seen.

"I suppose you are wondering what happened tonight at Charlie Tipple's," coolly began Maxie Mansard. "Oh, it was just terrible...*that girl* is just so coarse. Oh, it just depresses me...and I fear things have only just begun."

"What's going on?" laughed Harry, "Is there a revolution brewing in the female nation?"

"Harry," steadily began Maxie with nearly imperceptibly narrowed eyes. Maxie then paused to allow the waiter to serve them their champagne. She took a very shallow sip of her wine and continued, "The problem is, I fear, that I am on the wrong side, and I must admit I have never felt more torn...." Maxie paused to take another sip of wine, "You see my dear little Lily, my mentoree...is quite out of control, as she is charging and neighing her way through her first year at college. So, I am for now in a most murky place...stuck between loyalties and honor and affection. But there is something more to this, and it is that *more* that has me the most disturbed. I know to my very bones that it is not Lily that Charlie Tipple is after, rather, it's me," Maxie then sighed lightly and took a delicate sip of champagne.

Both Harry and Maxie fell silent for a spell.

"Abby and I are not getting along these days,"

said Maxie with just a tinge of sadness.

"I know," returned Harry without his usual smugness.

"Has she said anything about me?" asked Maxie.

"No, only that she sensed a tension between the two of you," returned Harry.

"She didn't?" asked Maxie, surprised.

"No, Abby can be a pest, but she doesn't talk behind anyone's back," said Harry.

"I'm starting to avoid her a little," said Maxie.

"I know," said Harry.

"I do feel bad though," said Maxie.

"I know," said Harry.

"It is just that she's weird. Nothing for her is simply pretty or pleasant. She is always attaching *meaning* to absolutely everything, whereas, I want as many things as possible to be pretty and pleasant. And what makes it all the worst is that I can't hate her. I still find myself wanting to see her. It's the oddest thing. It's as if I do not like her; rather, I want her. Do you know what I mean?" asked Maxie.

"I know what you mean," said Harry.

Maxie rose and Harry rose with her. The night had ended, had aged. It was time to go.

Harry did not feel bad to see it end, rather, he felt tremendous relief, as nothing was better than an evening with an obvious ending.

"I'll give you a ride," said Maxie.

"Thanks," answered Harry.

The Magician (Melanie)

"Two wishes, Melanie. I offer you two wishes."

Melanie jumped. "Who are you?" she asked, terrified. Melanie recoiled deeply into the full cushions of her couch. "And how did you get in here?" Melanie grabbed a pillow and pulled it over her chest.

The old man slowly walked towards the couch. He looked over towards the jangling television. The television turned off.

"What do you want from me?" cried Melanie.

"No, my dear, it is I who is offering," calmly returned the man.

Melanie blinked.

The old man smiled.

Melanie studied the person before her, the person who seemed to have appeared out of thin air. He wore a charcoal-colored flannel suit, a white shirt, and a silk tie swirled with blues and greens. His hair was white-gray and was styled impeccably. His nails were manicured, and he wore a large silver ring on his right hand.

Aware of being studied, the gentleman smiled and walked towards the window, turning his back to the woman. "I am no monster," he said casually. "Not that it matters...."

"Two wishes, my dear Melanie...I'm offering you two wishes," repeated the man who seemed still more concerned with outside the window than inside the window.

Melanie tucked her stringy brown hair behind her ears and frowned. She was beginning to notice boredom in the man's voice. This touched her pride enough to calm her.

"My name is Jonathan," he said. "It's all quite simple really. I've come to grant you two wishes... all you have to do is ask them." The man studied his nails and turned his silver ring. "Well, my dear Melanie, do you have any ideas?"

Melanie bit her lower lip. "I want to know death," she said steadily and stood.

Jonathan, visibly surprised, turned away from the window and took a step forward towards Melanie. He opened his mouth to speak, lifted his right hand, and then paused. He re-studied the woman standing before him. Her skin was pale brown and clear—he could almost see a layer of the lightest down coat her cheeks. She was not tall, but her shoulders and chin were square and strong. Her fingers, though nervous and twined, were thin and regular. Jonathan lowered his hand. He noticed that she had swollen, red eyes. He also (though only fleetingly) noticed that her irises were mink-like; the brown was furry and sensual.

"I am an old man," began Jonathan. "I'm assuming this is not a request to die—*permanently*," he said with more strength.

Melanie remained silent and blinked.

Jonathan began to pace the apartment. "Did you decorate this yourself?" he asked. "Of course you did," he answered. "I don't know what I was thinking...all you young women of today do everything yourselves. I actually sort of like your couches...everyone picks white, but orange, orange is interesting."

As Jonathan waved his hands and walked his legs, Melanie stood still and watched him in amazement. He was as gorgeous as he was ancient; his limbs moved gracefully while his eyes and lips seemed jagged—crooked.

Suddenly, Jonathan stopped moving and clapped his hands. "I've got it!" he yelled.

Melanie widened her eyes and took in a deep breath.

Jonathan leaped onto the couch and stretched out into an exaggerated lounge. "Oh, I'm too much... it took a little longer than average...this was not, however, average...it'll work...." mumbled Jonathan, pleased with himself.

Melanie remained silent.

Jonathan shot up from the couch. "Boy, you're not much of a talker, are you?" he asked.

Melanie opened her mouth.

"No, no, no bother. I sort of like it," answered Jonathan.

Jonathan walked to the apartment door. "Well Melanie, I wish you happiness," he gaily said as he opened the door.

Melanie did not move.

Jonathan exited through the door and quietly shut it behind him. Melanie ran to the door and opened it. She jumped into the hallway, but she saw nothing. She ran to the stairs and heard footsteps. She started to go down the old wooden stairs when she realized the footsteps were Mrs. Logan's, her neighbor.

"Mrs. Logan!" yelled Melanie.

"Yes, Melanie honey?" breathlessly asked the old woman.

"Did you pass a man on the steps?" asked Melanie.

"What sort of man?" asked the old woman.

"An older man, very handsome, with a dark suit?"

"I wish I had," laughed the old woman. "You haven't broken up with William, have you?"

"No Mrs. Logan, Bill and I are still together," answered Melanie.

"Oh, I'm glad...that William is so nice...."

"My phone's ringing," interrupted Melanie, "I've

got to go."

"Good-bye Melanie. I'll be looking out for this distinguished gentleman of yours," happily yelled the old woman.

"Bye!" yelled Melanie as she ran back into her apartment.

Melanie ran to the ringing telephone. "Hello?" she asked, panting.

"Melanie, it's me."

"What's up, Bill?" asked Melanie, disappointed.

"Are we still on for tonight?" asked Bill.

Melanie hesitated.

"Melanie, what's going on? First you broke our date yesterday, and now...."

"Nothing's going on Bill; I'm just tired. Yes, of course, tonight is still on." Melanie was feeling hot and electric; Bill was too ordinary right now. Melanie wanted to see *him* again. While the memory of Jonathan was just moments old, it had become as ornate and lush as a first kiss. In an almost cross, choke-speak Melanie continued, "So, you want to meet me at the restaurant, or do you want to go over together?"

"I'll pick you up," he answered sadly, aware of his recent effect on Melanie. He had become a boring man.

"In a couple of hours?" asked Melanie.

"Sure," he answered.

"Okay, see you then," quickly answered Melanie.

"Wait," said Bill.

"What?" asked Melanie impatiently.

"I love you," said Bill.

Melanie paused and rubbed her eyes. "Love you too," she answered quietly.

"See you tonight," said Bill weakly.

"Okay, tonight, bye-Bill," replied Melanie.

Melanie pressed the phone against her stomach and then placed it down on her coffee table. Her eyes lowered, and her skin darkened.

She walked listlessly to her bedroom and slung herself over her un-made bed. Melanie's bedroom was a mess. As the sun fell, mist hovered in the clear, evening air, flooding her bedroom with bright, gray light. Melanie noticed how strange it felt to be illuminated by gray. It somehow made the colors of her piled up clothes, scattered magazines, and a lifetime of disorder glow and float. Melanie lifted up her arm and touched her wrist. Her veins were darkening. She sat up and re-studied the inside of her arm. It was no mistake. Her veins were growing deep ocean blue right before her eyes. The longer Melanie stared, the more she felt her veins. They felt slow and thick; her pulse seemed to fade away with each breath; it wasn't frightening or definite but quiet and sleepy like warm water and night reading. All this, however, sat just underneath the tongue—just below Melanie's farthest thought. Melanie stood up and wandered around her dusty and shaggy belongings. Everything was changing but only by translucent shades. Sheets of gray cellophane were being placed over the shadow box, one after another.

* * *

Melanie walked through her apartment and changed the space from day to night. She was dressed, smoothed and lightly perfumed. Her limbs, now cared for and considered, were draped in thin burgundy wool. Her dark hair shined against her powdered cheeks. The smells of perfume and shampoo filled her one bedroom apartment. When she craved to taste her beauty again, to return to her mirror and re-smudge her lips with wine-colored lipstick, Bill knocked. He said she looked beautiful. She lowered her head and smiled. He put his gloves in his pocket. She put her gloves on. He suggested a restaurant. She said, *Sure.* She then suggested an alternative, and he said, *Fine.* As these everyday complexities prattled on, Melanie's skin continued to darken. Her veins were changing from ocean to night. Bill almost noticed, but then became sidetracked by an obscure memory. By the time the memory had fleeted, Bill had readjusted to Melanie's darkening.

They traveled to the restaurant on foot. The city was damp and freshly darkened. Bill admired the stretches of red and yellow light streaking and bouncing across Melanie's eyes. Smells of food and the pale backs of women in restaurants attracted Melanie's attention—air packed with roasted meat and browning butter, backs streaked with blue satin and brown wood.

Bill gently tapped Melanie's shoulder. Melanie

slowed and smiled. Across the street, the chosen bistro glowed with brightly colored paintings, shimmering patches of blond, and white coats. Bill touched her on the small of her back. Melanie stepped out into the street. Black wool and red lacquer pulsed through the aisles of the restaurant. A loud screech, the opening of a scream, silence. Melanie lay dead on the wet asphalt. Lights and people gathered. Bill walked backward for the rest of the night.

* * *

Between witnessing Melanie's death and attending her funeral, Bill was amazed by how often he received a memory, how many times he opened a door, how many times he addressed a person by their first name, how many times he went to the bathroom, and how many times he drank a drink. He just couldn't believe how much ordinary life would just flow right along after seeing her nearly decapitated head bleeding out torrents on the halted city street. Luckily for him, it was the day of the funeral, and all this life, all this movement could once again stop. His mother dressed him, his father answered the phone, and his parents drove him to the service.

Everything on days of funerals is brief and quiet. This is what was on Bill's dad's mind as he pulled into the funeral home parking lot.

Should I have made an extra casserole for

Melanie's father to freeze? This is what was on Bill's mom's mind as they stepped into the darkened room with shell-pink torchiers and a stunned mourning-screen.

I'm never going to this tailor again. This is what was on Johnathan's mind as he listened to the eulogy and pulled on the cuffs of his gray suit.

After the service, Jonathan followed everyone out to the cemetery. The day was cool and bright. Jonathan parked his black Mercedes several yards away from the other cars. He sat in his car and smoked as he watched the sad faces move up a low hill to the mausoleum. He nodded in appreciation as the casket rhythmically bobbed forward.

As soon as everyone was inside, Jonathan started up the hill. His blue eyes locked onto every grave he passed. As he reached the doors of the mausoleum, a young man, notably uncomfortable, stepped outside. Jonathan debated whether or not he should turn around and return to his car. The young man pulled out a pack of cigarettes and started to search his pockets.

"Hey, you got a light?" the young man asked with a nervous warmth.

Jonathan raised an eyebrow.

The young man with large brown eyes and freckles lifted both his eyebrows.

"Oh, yes, I'm sorry," said Jonathan in a polite drawl as he pulled out a slender gold lighter.

"Thanks," said the young man as he bent down towards the flame. "Pretty heavy, huh?" said the young man.

"Pardon?" asked Jonathan, whose eyes had returned to lasering the graves.

"I don't know how Uncle Davie even made it here today," returned the young man.

"Uncle Davie?" asked Jonathan.

"Melanie's dad," said the young man.

"Ah," returned Jonathan.

"I'm Melanie's cousin," said the young man.

"Oh," returned Jonathan.

"Jesus, this is just too weird," said the young man.

Jonathan, with feigned sincerity, spoke, "How so?"

"Well, with her mom just a week ago," the young man paused. Jonathan had turned his lasers onto the young man's face.

"Her mom?" asked Jonathan quietly.

"You mean Melanie didn't say anything to you? Ah, but that girl can be so tight-lipped. I remember...."

"Her mom died a week ago?" asked Jonathan, interrupting the young man.

"Are you a friend of hers from work?" asked the young man.

Jonathan, without answering, quickly turned around and walked back to his car. He sat in his car, smoked cigarettes, and listened to Bach until the sky grew exhausted of light and sunk into the soil.

* * *

"This is what I cannot understand, my dear

Melanie. Why did you pick knowledge of death over the return of your mother?" asked Jonathon. "I placed no limitation on my wishes. Why not wish her back?"

Melanie shot up from her television induced lull. She stared at the melted pink ice-cream in front of her and then down onto her gray sweat pants. "I'm back," she whispered. "I remember everything... we're back to the day...the day...I saw you...here... now...my wish." Melanie rose her heavy brown eyes to Jonathan. "How did you know about my mother?" she asked coldly.

"I went to your funeral," answered Jonathan with a smile.

"Leave," replied Melanie.

"Oh dear, oh dear, you see Melanie, I can't leave just yet... the second wish...remember you have one more to make."

"I want to be alone," answered Melanie.

Jonathan softened his expression and moved to the couch. "Okay, I'll leave you, for now, but just tell me what is death like?" asked Jonathan with a crippled and rusty tenderness.

"Look, Bill is calling soon, and I really need to rest. Please leave," pleaded Melanie whose eyes had grown heavier with each word.

Jonathan confidently turned his blue lasers on. Melanie remained steady, blinking. "Melanie, introduce me to death," he said while pouring his blue eyes into hers. Melanie lowered her lids, still unmoved.

Jonathan shuddered. Never before had his lasers not found an end. Her mink brown eyes were as infinite as his blue lasers.

"How is it that you can give me knowledge that you yourself do not know?" asked Melanie.

Jonathan turned off his lasers and stood up. "Priests do it every day," he growled through gritted teeth.

"Let me rest," creaked Melanie softly.

Jonathan scratched the top of his feathery head and pursed his lips. "Very well, my dear Melanie. I will return at a later date. Hopefully, you will be better rested and better spirited."

Melanie stared at the large, glowing plate-glass window of her living room as she listened to Jonathan walk to the door and leave.

* * *

Melanie, once again, agreed to *out* and prepared for *out*. The day was repeating the same day that she had died on with only subtle variations. Bill knocked as she was turning on lamps and shutting shades. She noticed that his hair was still wet and little bits of shaved beard were stuck to his neck. Bill took off his brown leather gloves and put them in his pocket. Melanie put on her coat. The coat felt heavier and smelled stronger than usual. She could smell cigarettes, skin, and traffic on the collar.

"Bill, does this coat smell?" asked Melanie.

Bill leaned over Melanie and smelled the back

of her neck. "No, I can just smell a little bit of your perfume."

Melanie frowned. They left. Once again, they traveled to the bistro on foot. Bill, however, was not studying the light in Melanie's eyes this time but was struck by a memory, the same memory that had struck him the last time he picked-up Melanie. The memory was obscure. It was him when he was four. He was at his Aunt Elaine's for the day. He had gone down into her storm cellar, and there he saw an entire wall lined with jarred peaches and pickled vegetables. He remembered studying the jars and staring at their faded, blurry contents. As he examined the jars on the shelf, he swore he saw something move inside of one of the jars. He instantly ran back upstairs. As soon as he saw his Aunt Elaine coming towards him, asking him, "What was the matter?" he wet his pants. This memory struck Bill as odd, because while he knew this was a factual history, this was the first time it had bubbled up as a memory.

As Melanie walked, she seemed less concerned with the smells of food and the backs of women. This time, sound filled her head. She felt as though she could hear each car pass individually, she could hear the music they were playing and the conversations they were having. She could hear dishes being washed and cats crying—even the stoplights seemed to send off a peculiar click. Bill's shoes made a gravelly sound, her coat almost crackled, all the buildings creaked, and the streetlights hummed.

Melanie took a deep breath and rubbed her forehead. "Bill, take me home," said Melanie.

"Take you home?" asked Bill.

"Walk me home," repeated Melanie.

Bill paused and stared at Melanie. He slowly reached out his arm towards her. She lowered her chin and eyes.

"I want to go home," she said.

Bill said nothing, shrugged his shoulders, and turned around.

"Thank you," said Melanie.

As they walked back to Melanie's apartment, Bill wrapped his long arm around her shoulders and occasionally leaned over and kissed the top of her fragrant head.

Bill walked her up to her fourth-floor apartment and stopped at the door. Melanie pulled out her keys and opened the door. The hall was dimly lit with an old wall sconce that at one time was nice. A couple of people carrying filled paper bags could be heard chatting as they walked up the wooden stairs. Bill leaned over and kissed Melanie tenderly on her forehead.

"Good night, Melanie," he said softly.

Melanie, surprised, looked up at Bill. His green eyes were round and filled with a fatigued love; his neck, long and slender, was blotched with crimson patches; and as always, his clothes were tidy and muted. Guilt rose to her mouth. "Aren't you going to come in?" she asked.

Bill smiled warmly and shook his head. "I know

you want to be alone," he answered.

Melanie smiled meekly and pushed her door wide open. "I love you," she said.

"I love you," said Bill.

"I'll call you," offered Melanie.

Bill nodded silently, turned, and walked away. Melanie watched him disappear and stepped into her apartment.

* * *

The next day, Melanie woke up with a vague sense of being over-filled. The watery morning light filled her bedroom and turned her closed eyelids pink. Melanie began her rolling and moaning, thinking and deciding. Blue skirt, cream sweater: "No, I feel bloated." Brown pants, pink top, brown jacket: "No, too hot." Red skirt, red jacket, little lizard purse: "Too red, way too red," Powder-blue pants, powder-blue, turtleneck sweater: "Perfect, I'll feel comfortable."

Melanie pulled her body out of bed and into her tiny bathroom. Dozens of possible outfits lined the floor of the room. A thick fall of towels in various stages and sizes hung off the back of the door, and several eye shadows, some ancient, some new, waited on the back of the toilet. As Melanie waded and washed, dried and combed, squinted and dusted, the sounds, smells, and even the measured rolling of time pinched her senses, making her nerves redden. Her jaw grew rubbery as her attention magnified.

As Melanie walked to work, she sucked in deeply the damp morning air. Her chest would tighten with each over-recognized breath. She could detect subtle differences in yeast and exhaust; she could smell the oxygen and water in the air. But with each tense pull of air into her chest, she gave herself a reason to be thankful: Bill was high on her list for things to be grateful for (this surprised her). She used her job once, then chuckled out of embarrassment. Her apartment was a big one. Her health was one which she used twice. She tried to use her loving parents, but the thought only gave her a choking sensation.

* * *

Much to Melanie's relief, her walk home from work was crowded and peaceful. Her hunger kept her thoughts earthy and centered. Her mouth watered, and her stomach churned as she thought of all the possibilities for dinner. As she hopped up the stairs, her nostrils quivered. The most fragrant scents of butter and wine filled the building. As Melanie neared her door, she realized the smells were coming from her apartment.

"What is Bill up to?" she whispered as she unlocked her door and entered.

Melanie took two steps into her apartment and froze. Soft jazz effortlessly fluttered through the fragrant air. Vanilla candles in thick glass pots were placed on every flat surface along with glass jars of fragile spring flowers. Thin layers of smoke and crackling sounds floated out from the kitchen and rested above the couch. And Jonathan, wearing black wool slacks, a white shirt, and an apron stood in the middle of the living room, holding two foggy martinis.

"Come in, come in, come in, I made you a martini," said Jonathan excitedly.

"What's all this?" asked Melanie, surprised.

"Dinner, darling. I've noticed you haven't had one in a while. Oh Melanie, just shut the door and grab a martini," said Jonathan.

Melanie slowly moved towards Jonathan and took the drink from his out-stretched arm.

"This is delicious," she said.

Jonathan rose his eyebrows and shook his head approvingly. "Wait until you try my cooking," he said, beaming with pride.

Melanie handed Jonathan back her glass. It was empty and still ice-cold.

"Another?" asked Jonathan.

Melanie smiled with her eyes and shook her head *yes*. "I'll be back in a minute," she said kindly.

Melanie turned on the light of her bedroom and dropped her jaw. All the drawers were shut, her bed was made, and she could see polished wood and vacuumed carpet on the floor. Melanie took off her coat and draped it over the bed. She cautiously tip-toed to her dresser and opened a drawer. Her clothes were clean, pressed, and neatly folded. Quickly, as if opening a present, she opened all the drawers.

"I can't relax in the midst of absolute chaos,"

said Jonathan.

Melanie jumped and touched her chest. “You scared me,” she said. “You did all this?”

Jonathan nodded his head. “This is nothing. You should see your bathroom,” he said proudly.

Melanie tossed her purse on her bed and ran to the bathroom. “It’s so clean...where is everything?”

“You do own a linen closet. I believe I’m leaning against it,” said Jonathan with a whimsical smile.

“I can’t believe all this,” said Melanie.

Melanie walked past Jonathan through her glowing living room and entered the kitchen. Jonathan quietly followed her.

“Dinner will be ready momentarily,” he said. “Here, take your martini.”

Melanie took the drink and leaned against the counter with wide, happy eyes. “Do you want any help?” she slurped with her glass on her lips.

“You can set the table. I took the liberty of buying you some linens...I simply cannot bear paper napkins.”

Melanie took the white linen bundle off the counter and proceeded to dress the table.

“We’ll need two forks,” said Jonathan mechanically as he pulled a tray out of the oven.

Melanie finished the table. She felt drunk and happy.

“Ready?” asked Jonathan proudly.

Melanie shook her head.

“Oh, the wine, Melanie, will you pull out the wine from the refrigerator?”

Melanie pulled out a bottle of white wine. "This one?" she asked.

"No, that's the Sauterne. Grab the one on the door," answered Jonathan.

Melanie pulled out the chardonnay. "So, you want me to open and pour?" she asked.

"No, you sit down," answered Jonathan. "Oh wait, you can, however, grab some candles and flowers from the other room."

"Oh yeah," said Melanie excitedly.

Melanie placed three little potted candles on the table and an olive jar with its label soaked off filled with lily of the valley, fresh sprigs of sage, and rosemary. The effect was mesmerizing. Melanie gazed around her little, white kitchen. "I can't believe this is my apartment," she said.

Jonathan poured the wine and placed a beautiful, intricate creation in front of her.

"This looks amazing," said Melanie, beaming.

Jonathan dimmed the lights and sat down across from her.

"I don't even want to touch it; it looks so good," said Melanie.

"It's potato pancakes with smoked salmon and dill cream," said Jonathan.

Jonathan waited for Melanie to start. Melanie cautiously sliced into a triangular wedge of pancake and topped her piece with a sliver of salmon and a dollop of creme fraiche loaded with fresh dill, white pepper, and lemon. "This is unbelievable," she howled. Each flavor soaked her tongue, ringed her throat, and arose with her breaths.

"Oh, my god Jonathan, I've never tasted anything like it."

"Thank you," returned Jonathan who also seemed to be enjoying his work.

Melanie cleared her plate and sat deeply back in her chair. Jonathan, who had barely finished half of his, instantly stood up, catching his napkin right before it hit the floor.

"Ready for course number two?" he asked.

Melanie beamed. "Bring it on."

The rest of the dinner flowed like colored ribbons. The second course was a bowl of hot-acid orange, sweet pepper bisque decorated with parsley and paprika. Melanie moaned. The third course was pan-fried lamb chops girdled with a chevre compote and a deep brown morel sauce. Each bite swirled around Melanie's head and made her drunk. The fourth course was light and refreshing; Melanie chewed her baby greens with pleasure. The fifth course came with a pause. Melanie was full of pleasure and *thank yous* as Jonathan cleared away plates and made coffee. John Coltrane swam around the kitchen, biting Melanie's toes and licking her cheeks. The candles, flowers, seared fat of lamb, and coffee poured Melanie's senses into her chest. Melanie swooned.

Jonathan poured the Sauterne—oily and honeysuckle sweet—and the coffee. Melanie felt herself consuming, panting, and rocking. The fifth course was a tender strawberry tart that hovered weightlessly above a pool of jet black, chocolate-cranberry sauce.

"I can't believe all this. I can't believe how it's all affecting me," said Melanie as she finished her last bite.

"Pardon me?" asked Jonathan. This was the most he had ever heard Melanie say.

"Your dinner Jonathan...it's as though I've never eaten in my life...that is, before tonight," answered Melanie.

"Perhaps this was your first *meal,*" offered Jonathan.

"But the alcohol, even the alcohol is affecting me differently...I feel hot, alive...everything is so electric," she returned as she poured herself another bowl of Sauterne.

"Really?" asked Jonathan, genuinely curious.

Melanie nodded and stood up. "I can still taste everything. I *tasted* everything. The lamb was seared in rendered pork fat and peanut oil. White pepper—not black—was used in the bisque. And you used a touch of fresh rosemary in the tart. I can taste *everything.*"

Jonathan pinched his temple and stared at Melanie. He wanted desperately to ask Melanie of death, but he stuffed his wish into his leathery fist.

"Let's go out," said Melanie feverishly.

"Out?" asked Jonathan who was still holding tightly onto his wish. He had never been asked to grant knowledge of death, and now that someone had, he burned with the desire to know. It had been countless, *countless* years since he had been so hotly consumed with desire.

"Dancing, drinking, smoking, I want to go move in the dark," said Melanie as she tore out of the kitchen. "Come on, Jonathan."

Jonathan stood up and followed her with an unaccustomed speed. Melanie was growing into an intricate, tempting, spinning mystery.

"What's all this about?" asked Jonathan with a voice he hadn't used naturally in years.

Jonathan turned the corner and found Melanie standing on top of her bed wearing only her sweater and a pair of pink cotton panties.

"You need black and gel," howled Melanie as she tore off her sweater and flung it across the room.

Jonathan leaned against the doorjamb and smiled. "Moi?" he asked with a feigned severity.

"Oui," purred Melanie. She then leaped off her bed and tore into her dresser. She bent and moved unconsciously like an animal. Melanie's dresser sang off jerks and clicks as Melanie tossed through it. A black sweater twirled through the air and landed on Johnathan's shoulder.

"Good toss," said Jonathan excitedly.

"Slip it on," said Melanie as she tore off her pink, cotton underwear and replaced them with a black lace pair.

Jonathan excitedly unbuttoned his shirt, stared at Melanie, and sighed. Jonathan knew he could no longer truly decipher between love and exciting entertainment; however, as Melanie sat on the floor and strung up her black stockings, he realized that at the moment the difference did not matter.

Melanie disappeared into her closet and came out wearing a pair of black leather shorts and a pair of black leather riding boots.

"Amazing," whispered Jonathan.

"Top, top, I need a perfect top," frantically sang Melanie. Melanie leaped back to her dresser. Clothes flew. A snug, black cashmere t-shirt landed on her chest.

"What do you think?" childishly asked Melanie with locks of brown hair over her eyes.

"Satanic," answered Jonathan.

"Gel time," yelled Melanie as she whizzed past Jonathan. "You too, Jonathan."

Jonathan followed her to the bathroom and stood behind her.

She sprayed, fluffed, and teased. She smudged her eyes with black and stained her lips red. Her brown irises turned to deep velvet, and her sand-colored skin turned to matte silk. "You're next," she said as she turned around.

Melanie paused. Her face almost brushed against his chin. He was old, very old, but he was as handsome as he was aged. His handsome, however, was not polished wood or fine leather but the handsome found in wicked old trees and horse's legs.

Jonathan, in the most exciting state of agony he'd felt in years, took a step back.

Melanie blushed and smiled. "I want to do your hair," she said shyly.

Jonathan smiled like a softened mercenary. "Do as thou wilt," he returned.

Johnathan's hair was thicker than Melanie had imagined it would be.

* * *

Melanie's capacity for drink was greater than Jonathan had imagined. To move through the dark is what Melanie wanted, and move through the dark was what they did. Melanie hard-swayed in and out of shadows to loud, angry music. She chewed drink after drink, grinned as she exhaled smoke, and slapped the roof of Johnathan's Mercedes as he sped her around the city. Jonathan laughed and shook his head while Melanie whistled about work, food, and sex.

* * *

At dawn, the city can weigh more than all the oceans together. Jonathan pulled into an empty parking lot and turned off the engine. Tears welled up in Melanie's eyes. Jonathan lit a cigarette.

"It's time Melanie...it's time you make your second wish," said Jonathan with genuine sadness. This was all the time he would get with her. This was all the time he ever got with people.

Melanie tore out of the car. Jonathan glanced at the tarnished ring on his right hand. "Damn you," he whispered with clenched teeth. Jonathan slammed the steering wheel with his hands and shot out of the car. His lit cigarette fell out of his mouth and rolled onto the faded pavement.

"Melanie!" he yelled. "Melanie, wait," yelled Jonathan as he stammered down the sidewalk.

Melanie stopped. Jonathan stopped. In the early morning light, Melanie appeared not as a woman but as an oriental screen decorated with tiny birds and turning fish.

"What is behind that damned screen?" moaned Jonathan as he slowly walked towards Melanie, feeling the age of the world and the age of his legs.

The two met on the empty sidewalk. Neither was ready for sleep.

"I could end hunger or request world peace," said Melanie with tears in her eyes.

"You could," gulped Jonathan.

Melanie gazed down at Johnathan's hands. They appeared old and shaky. It was the first time he looked human to her. Jonathan self-consciously ran his fingers through his thick silver hair.

Melanie started to talk and then paused. Jonathan touched his gnarled silver ring. "Your wish Melanie, it's time," he said with a decayed compassion.

"I want it gone," stuttered Melanie. "I want my knowledge of death to be erased," she said with tears slipping out of the charcoaled corners of her eyes. "I know it's selfish. I know I could do something good for the world, but what I want is for this knowledge to be erased."

Jonathan shut his eyes for a few seconds. He would have to remain unrequited until the very rare and odd chance someone else would request knowledge of death. Though somehow, he knew even if another did request to have this knowledge, it would not be the same understanding of death Melanie saw. He wanted Melanie's knowledge of death, and this made things far worse for him, as he would never see her again. "Very well," he said softly. And with that, Jonathan turned around and walked back to his car. Melanie started to follow but realized this was their time to part. She remained still until Jonathan climbed into his shiny black whale and slid away.

The Business
(Jessica)

Jessica surveyed her surroundings. She hadn't intended on taking her independence this far, but now that she was standing in the middle of the mall parking lot, she realized that her trembling exhilaration had more to do with pride than fear. Queasy images of her having to lie to strangers, telling them that they were traveling and got robbed, and now needed gas money to get home. She thought of the constant moves and the myriad of drug buddies her parents insisted she refer to as "uncle." Everything in her parents' life was so stained, dishonest, and worn. She was always being sucked into their rotting abyss. However, throughout her entire young life, she always sensed that this grimy existence was not to be her existence. She knew there was something out there for her—she sensed she had a kind of saving grace. And she did—and it had to do with what she was made of.

Jessica was completely gold-colored—head to toe. She was not very big, but her ocean of gold light swung an aura of largeness around her child-like features. She was eighteen and had decided right then and there to get out of the car and refuse to get back in. It felt as though water had finally reached her dying tongue when she jumped out of the car. It was the first time she felt total, complete agency. She thought of constantly having to change the diapers making sure her siblings had clothes to wear for school in the morning. She even had to check and mind the mouse traps, rat traps, roach traps, and spray the constant lava of ants that seemed to follow her and her family around like a shimmering black ghost. Cars filled with people were buzzing around her, but they could not be seen. The blinding gold shower of Jessica's presence drowned out everything, transforming the parking lot into a vast desert. Jessica never felt more clear or powerful than at that moment (and that was probably why rays of solid fire were beaming out of her flesh).

Jessica had met a kind of woman that she had never met before. It all began in a Greek restaurant. She and her best friend, Sara, were eating souvlaki sandwiches and drinking beers. They were thrilled out of their minds to have been served alcohol. They felt fiendish and alive. The owner of the restaurant was in his fifties and was pumping them with beers, dirty eyes, and tender, almost fatherly, compliments.

At first, the girls felt powerful, but as time slid by and the restaurant began to empty, the girls grew scared.

Jessica and Sara fled to the bathroom. They huddled over the toilet of the little one-room bathroom. They were scared. A woman started to knock then demanded that she gain entrance. Sara opened the door. The woman paused, thinking the girls would politely exit. But they didn't; the girls remained in their hover.

"What are you girls up to?" asked the woman. The woman had deep yellow hair and heavy makeup, and yet beneath the dyes, she was strikingly beautiful. She was in her late thirties, and she was wearing a black leather pantsuit with lush gold jewelry.

The girls together and with great animation braided their evening with strands of fancy, fear, and truth. The woman listened with a happy smile that appeared oddly natural, and by her wrinkles, this smile was also frequent. "Girls, you're hiding in the bathroom for just a couple of beers? Ah, honey, you don't owe him anything," she drawled lovingly.

The girls blinked.

"You've got some set of eyes on you," said the woman to Jessica.

"Thank you," said Jessica. She shivered. She had never been complimented by a full-grown woman, and it held a weight that draped over her body like a heavy fur coat.

The woman then bit her lower lip in thought. "I don't ordinarily do this," she began, "but I've got a feeling about you."

"Me?" excitedly asked Jessica.

The woman nodded her head and stroked her eyes over Jessica. "Have you ever thought about the business?" asked the woman.

Jessica and Sara stared blankly at the woman.

"*The business*," The woman blushed a bit and smiled widely. "Jesus, you could make a fortune."

Jessica gulped. She was beginning to understand. "You mean a prostitute?" asked Jessica nervously. Her armpits were soaked sponges. She could feel crimson blotches rise up her neck. This night was growing darker and scarier, and her regular life now seemed small and impossible.

"We just call it the business," answered the woman. "*At least in my line*."

Jessica shook her head unconsciously side to side.

"We would put you up in an amazing penthouse and dress you in clothes that you see on the catwalks of Paris," said the woman like a purring, mother cat.

"What about pimps and all that? Don't they beat you up and put you on drugs?" asked Jessica in an incredulous panic.

The woman shook her head side to side. "It's not like that...especially for girls like you...you get good grades, don't you?" returned the woman.

"Straight A's," bulleted Sara.

Jessica slashed an angry glance at Sara...it seemed that not even Sara was acting normal.

"Look, here is my card. Think about it. It's not

often I meet your variety...and trust me this is the place for your kind." The woman handed Jessica a cream-colored business card. "Now girls. I really must use the bathroom. I don't mind if you stay, but I think you would."

"Let's go," said Sara.

"Yeah," trailed Jessica.

"Now, remember girls just walk out...you don't *owe him anything.*"

The girls started to walk away. "Wait," said Jessica. Jessica trotted back to the bathroom. She softly knocked on the door.

"Someone's in here," hollered the woman.

"It's me...the girl," trembled Jessica.

There was no answer. Jessica could hear the toilet flush. Within seconds the door opened. The woman stared deeply, as if to hypnotize, into Jessica's eyes.

"What did you mean? What is my kind?" asked Jessica with excitement and sadness.

"You have so much glow and light that they will pay and pay and pay, trying desperately to soak into you and yet, no matter how many times they come and no matter how far they travel, they will never ever touch your ground. You will end with power... you see...when you are made entirely of gold, no matter how soft and traded, you will never tarnish... this is what *the business* has always been about... men trying to tarnish gold." The woman paused and again smiled with a smile that could make joy. "But the truth is, gold don't tarnish, and the men die coming, trading, and buying."

Jessica worked full time at Macy's department store. She was the only employed member of her family. She actually loved working there. It was a welcome contrast to her world of *barely-there-home*. She loved the strong air-conditioning and the constant smell of perfume. She loved the various displayed lifestyles throughout the different departments. They all were pure fantasy to her. She never had a reason to wear a workout outfit nor did she ever see a need to wear a long gown. Certainly, she had never worn lace underwear or a feather fringed satin robe. But she wanted to, and spending daily time with these frozen mannequin vignettes inspired her—and again, brought her directly into contact with her inner knowing that her world of sticky fingers, dirty cheeks, and stained boys' clothes was not going to be her world forever. It was not, and that *it was not* was a very close relative to genuine luxury, and Jessica knew it.

It was three in the afternoon on an intensely hot Saturday in May. The hot air smelled strongly of asphalt, as the heat was causing the ocean-sized parking lot to soften and weep. Jessica's parents in their huge Ford LTD station wagon growled and putt-putt-coughed outside the mall entrance. It was rusty brown colored and thickly covered in dust. It kicked off a strong odor of gasoline. Her parents and siblings barely acknowledged Jessica as she ran around the front of the vehicle. "Where is it?" demanded her father. His face was extremely sunburnt, and his gray and blond hair appeared wet he was sweating so much. You could tell that at one point he had been very handsome but now appeared all the worse for having lost it.

Jessica pulled a curdled bottle of milk out from her seat and eyed her eight-month-old sister. She hated the fact that her parents did not bother to feed the baby properly. It was not uncommon for the baby to be served old, curdled bottles found in the car and elsewhere. Jessica instinctively knew that it would mean the baby was doomed. She knew her sister was not going to ever thrive. But Jessica was just so tired of having to take care of everything and everyone. Her entire family was in the car. This made Jessica uneasy. It meant they were hiding. It meant danger, as most likely, her parents were unable to pay their dealer. Dad, five-year-old Ben, and mom were up front. Ten-year-old Robbie, baby Carrie Ann, and Jessica sat in the back seat. And fourteen-year-old Mark and twelve-year-old Jonathan were huddled in the very back along with several miscellaneous plastic bags.

Her father demanded she hand over her paycheck, but after she had handed the check to him, she made a spontaneous decision to get out of the car and know that this was it. She then pulled out that business card that to her had previously seemed completely black and impossible and decided to see if being made of gold also meant hope.

When the woman she met at the restaurant introduced Jessica to the beautiful penthouse and her *manager*, Jessica knew that she had entered a world in which she would never leave. But this did not frighten her...for she would possess this clamp. She would be fully committed to this world and make it her triumph and sanctuary. Her whole life had been of taking, of using, of wearing down, and now finally she was going to make something impeccable. She had sensed her whole young life that a vocation was to be her road—she knew she could make this spontaneous, black turn into a vocation. The manager was handsome, gay, and much older than Jessica imagined a man in his capacity would be. The woman who gave her the card turned out to be gay as well, and Jessica would break her virginity with her female scout the same night she was picked up outside the mall's Cineplex. Jessica enjoyed the sex immensely, but not particularly in a sexual way, rather in a scholarly way. In truth, Jessica was a student more than anything, and this character trait would bring her more power and money than she could have ever known the night she learned about clitorises and dildoes. She absorbed every movement and every word from her mentor.

As the months flew by, Jessica spent every moment of her off time studying. She watched hours of pornography, she poured through the society sections of several newspapers and magazines, and she also ventured deeper into the human-historical world of sex by studying shunga, medieval Japanese erotica, and the *Kamasutra*. She would experiment and perfect how to groom her watermelon colored diamond and how to dress its soft, metallic hair by combining ancient and modern preferences regarding the female valley. The money was heavy and fell over her like rain.

Within a year, Jessica would develop skill beyond measure. Her sides grew into taunt, fine animals that moved like deer in flight, and her kisses could tease out even the most ancient and crusted suffering from the heels of men. Her clients would orgasm so deeply and violently that immediately afterward, they would find themselves vomiting. Their naked bodies would lean against Jessica's toilet, in her crystal bathroom, and they would wonder if this was a natural function of the human body. When they would string up their neckties and calculate how much they owed Jessica, they would always get the haunting feeling that the money they gave her had everything to do with her power and not theirs.

After three decades of impeccability, Jessica left her post at the penthouse. When she had first entered that penthouse, she intuited that she would never leave it, and indeed she was correct. As she lived quietly away from the world of the business, her impeccability regarding the business did not leave her. That world, the world of the business, remained in her every smile, in all of her pleasant conversations at church, and in the way she walked across a room. There was a sphere of untouchability that always surrounded her, and it kept her happy and lonely and pure. The small town where she had moved was left brokenhearted, as she never acquiesced to any advances (and of course there were many) but not enough to abandon her, as she was always told, "Good morning, good evening, and hello," right up to her death. They threw her a very sweet and kind funeral. The reception was at a widower's house. The gentleman was a member of the church where both had attended. He had loved Jessica greatly and had taken care of her in the last days of her illness. And he missed her even though their meeting had put him in a painful prison of his affection.

The woman was correct about Jessica. No matter how much they came, bought and traded, they could not make gold tarnish.

"Get in the car!" yelled her father. "Jessica, get in the goddamned car now!" However, Jessica did not follow her father's orders. He did pause to see if she would turn, but soon enough, she had re-entered Macy's large, glass-doored entrance. He wanted to get out, park, and get her then beat her as hard as he could. But he could not, as he had to get the paycheck cashed as soon as he could, so he could pay their dealer and get more for the weekend. Luckily, his wife had always signed the endorsement, so he did not need Jessica very much anyway. Deep down, he knew she was gone and that he and the rest of the family were all very much doomed without her. He actually felt a few tears rise in his eyes as he drove off knowing she was gone. He felt sorry for himself and felt as though his daughter was completely cold-hearted to have abandoned him and the rest of the family. He thought on several occasions that evening and throughout the rest of his life that Jessica, his oldest, turned out to be very selfish. He would often boast that *Jessica is dead to me.*

Back in the mall with its air conditioning and fantasy, Jessica felt born again. Finally, she had come into her long-sensed inheritance. She was never going back to that life or those people again. The Universe had spoken and had given her an escape from an unexpected quarter. She did walk a few laps around the mall's interior drag before she went to a payphone at the mall's Cineplex. Her hand and wrist were shaking when she pulled the business card out of her little, red vinyl wallet. Her palms and feet began to sweat profusely. Before calling she sat down on a large circular planter that was tiled in a multi-colored abstract pattern with red, orange, and blue being the primary colors. The cool tile felt nice on her hands as she pressed her palms down. The business card, now feeling more like a piece of cotton cloth, was between her palm and the tile. She then thought of her doomed baby sister Carrie Ann and stood.

The Tao

Well It Matters (Jennifer)

Everything began with me watching television. I was jumping channel to channel, looking hopefully for a documentary-style show on someone losing tons of weight, possibly about fashion models and all the things they do in a day and evening, or (my third favorite type of television show—this list was in order of preference) a documentary movie on something that will make me want to do all sorts of meaningful things like the movie I recently saw (*Cook Your Life*) that had me briefly checking out retreats at Californian Buddhist monasteries. With my cable package that I pay for monthly, I have around six different PBS stations with one of them being this kind of mega PBS called PBS *World*. Now, if you are not from America, PBS is our "public broadcasting station" and claims to be "viewer supported" and committed to all kinds of excellence etc. Maybe you have something like this in your country: a television station where no one is tan or good looking, where somehow there is a never-ending demand for Dixieland jazz, and where everybody either lives on lovely or bleak farms or in lovely or bleak city apartments but never in a tract house unless it is a show about how awful tract houses are for the environment and the community (and PBS loves loves loves using words like *environment, community,* and *outreach*). And yet, sometimes there are some good shows. One good show is *Frontline*. *Frontline* is this ultra-super-serious television show with this voice-over guy that is amazing. I have never seen a picture of him, but that voice just brings the whole doom and terribleness of whatever topic they are covering to life. So, *Frontline* is this documentary television series that picks a super awful topic and scares the crap out of you for an hour or so. Now, when I was looking for a weight loss television show, I found myself briefly landing on PBS right in the middle of *Frontline*. This *Frontline* was "The Digitalization of America" (something like that). And as I paused on the channel and listened to that unbelievably effective voice-over voice, we quickly find ourselves in a lab. There is a bubbly young boy (around three years old) and a youngish lady in a white lab coat. The two are huddled around a computer, and the boy is happy and jumpy, and the woman is sufficiently maternal in her overall demeanor. And for now, the voice-over voice is all quiet, and we are left simply with the ambient sounds of the lab. After a few seconds of this bucolic (propaganda) scene of the happy to be scientifically tested three-year-old boy and the kind, Madonna figure in her white, laboratory coat, we are seamlessly spliced over to a very small windowless room with one man's back to us and one man's face to us. Both men appeared to be the same kind of liberal, microbrewery, running, corduroy wearing men of thirty-five to forty-five. These men could easily be trapped in large numbers on any weekend at REI, and if I were Godzilla or King Kong and were looking to lower my cholesterol and perhaps shed a view terror-slowing pounds, I would go there and really pig out, because all of these men have wives that shop at Whole Foods grocery store and prepare ultra-organic, locally produced, developing world-inspired dishes that are so unbelievably good for you, one no longer has to trouble with God. (Note: you will be gassy after eating loads of people at REI; however, I can only imagine that being an asset in your line of work.) Anyway, the one whose back is to us is the interviewer, and the one facing us is the scientist who we quickly realize is the mastermind behind the previous scene depicting (clearly) America's new idyllic paradigm of women and children. So it seems that this scientist has found that when young children are virtually exposed to events (like virtually eating a taco or virtually surfing with dolphins) later on in life, most (or *many*—I cannot wholly remember) of the children thought they literally had done those virtual activities. Essentially, if you expose little kids to virtual experiences, there is a really good chance that later on, their brains will not be able to distinguish those activities from any real-life activities they had also experienced. This is spooky stuff—especially if you grew up in America watching *Frontline* on PBS, and you were assigned in school to read George Orwell's 1984 (as I was my freshman year in high school). So, within seconds, my mind was racing over all sorts of dangerous possibilities combining happy to be lab tested three-year-olds and happy to test motherly lab technicians and a very subtle totalitarian regime. Luckily, or surprisingly, the interviewer kind of blurted out "Really?" "Is that good for them?" "I mean, is there any kind of possibility of harm here?" Then, and I will never forget this, never, and I will have much more to say and do regarding this, but for now I simply will give you the scientist's reply: "Well, it really does not concern me. I mean, not from the perspective of my work. And you know, that is where we are heading, so it does not really matter." Now, note that this is a paraphrase and that I am profoundly too lazy and undisciplined as a writer to go online and find the verbatim actual quote, but I know this is pretty close, because I am still super pissed off by it. (Plus, I am billing this mess as fiction—which I promise will commence shortly.) In fact, I was so mad that I had to turn the television off in complete horror and outrage at what kind of world we were collectively building. Now, besides thinking mind-programming innocent, just out of the box humans is okay, thinking it is okay, because "that is where things are heading" is total decadence. It is time for someone to perhaps lay off the Indonesian stir-fries and special winter ambers and perhaps do a little moral inventory.

Now, I am by all reasonable assessments a nobody, and generally speaking, years of solitude and minimal resistance develops just the kind of nobody that I am (which is like a cracked patch of sidewalk). (Thank you, Chuang Chou!) Now, if you couple this cracked patch of sidewalk beingness with my time-consuming commitments of television watching and hanging out in my kitchen with friends and beverages, well, I find myself in no real position to go to this scientist and like some great nineteenth-century evangelist get him to see the light. The best and only real thing I can do is make up a story about him. So, at least I could virtually experience a world with a little more justice.

Now, we're going to begin this story in Ithaca, NY where our scientist (the scientist mentioned above) lives with his wife of five years and four-year-old twins: a boy named Gilroy and a girl named Plum. Gilroy and Plum were well into their first year at the local, experimental co-op day school (with very generalized age to skill guidelines). So far so good, excepting that since the twins have been attending The Mountain Tail Cooperative Learning Center and Imagination Refuge, they have been seemingly permanently stained with the smell of apple cider, and it appears that no amount of bathing and clothes washing can get the two smelling like kids again.

Our scientist, Don, had been under a lot of pressure as of late, because while he was a full-fledged Ph.D. from Stanford, his post-doctoral fellowship at Cornell was just barely paying the bills. He had secretly hoped that his wife Leanne would have sensed the money situation and suggest that maybe she should look for something part-time (at least), for Leanne actually did have a degree in journalism from Stanford. But alas, it seemed paradoxical (to him—moms know otherwise) that now that the twins were finally in school, she was busier than ever with the twin business. Ithaca too was growing problematic. Leanne had them wrapped up in so many cooperatives and committees that it seemed there were always men with beards and sweaters and women that touch their face and your arm a lot when they spoke in his kitchen drinking herbal teas and saying things like "action plan" and "people need to know." I mean, Don saw himself as a good man and that part of being a good man was to be on committees that told other people how to be better or how good people do it or what bad people were currently doing to stupid people. But Don also saw himself as worldly and pessimistic and that once someone had reached his level of perspective, one really could not be held to the same good, liberal guy standards. I mean, Don sometimes ate steaks and sometimes engaged in violent video games and sometimes felt that female scientists were in some ways not intrinsically capable of being great scientists (even though Don was on the Math For Girls Now Action Committee).

Luckily for Don, an offer to come out and interview for a tenure-track position at Perdue had come his way. And things were looking really good, as he had already cleared the initial CV review and telephone interview process, and they were going to pay for his flight to Indiana—his hotel room, food—everything. Now, while this Don story is fiction, I am somewhat required as the writer (even if absolutely everything is totally made-up) to come up with fairly reasonable actions and reactions. I mean, while I can suddenly put Don in a wheelchair or cause a great flood to wash away all of Ithaca, I would still have to provide a reasonable sequence getting you there. Likewise, with internal decisions like say, for the purposes of my story, I need Don to choose to drive to Indiana instead of taking the free flight. This seems difficult to believe, so here is the tricky part of fiction: I need to make up a believable reason for Don to decide to drive instead of fly. And I will, but before I do, I will also include another weird aspect of fiction: while yes, I am making up all sorts of things in this story, I am telling you a lot of real things too. I actually lived in Ithaca while my husband completed both his Ph.D. in toxicology and a post-doctoral fellowship at Cornell. And while I will say absolutely, positively that my husband is nothing like Don, I have during my tenure in Ithaca met and endured many a dinner with the Scientist Dons of the world, so know, just know. Also, in the big heat of summer, my dog was dying. Simultaneously, my husband was asked to be a groomsman for a friend's wedding in Lafayette, Indiana. So, the vet told me either he could put her down, or I could take her and let her die at home. I decided to take her home. Our car had no air conditioning, so we left for Indiana at night, thinking my poor, dying dog would be more comfortable as she drifted away in the back seat of our car. Oddly, by the time we made it to Indiana, our dog was more conscious than not, and finally, by the time we returned to Ithaca, she was completely fine. It was a very weird thing to do—to drive all night with a nearly dead dog in the back seat in the incredible openness of that region. The best beers I ever had were the ones we had when we finally made it to our little motor lodge in Indiana. We sipped very cold Budweisers while watching the local news as my dog was walking in and out of the bathroom to drink from the toilet (which, by the way, was one of the best sounds I had ever heard—I would give anything to hear her slurp in her loud, messy moose way just one more time, as she has since passed away). Anyway, my whole point is that while I am seriously making this all up, I am seriously telling the truth, and this is the best thing and the most rotten thing about fiction, because everyone I know and do not know will get the two confused, and I will have to say "No, I wasn't talking about *you*" and

"Mom, it's *fiction.*"

So, Don decided to drive to Indiana, because A. he wanted to take his beloved, though thoroughly resented, car: a 1989 Saab 900 turbo convertible that he purchased used with little knowledge of cars and what makes cars reliable. The problem was that Leanne still had to haul her and the twins around in her old Honda Civic from her Stanford days, and what she really needed was a Toyota Prius. However, the only way they could afford this karma friendly trade-up was if they sold both of their old cars. But the thing was, even though the Saab was not very good at vim and vigor; it was the car Don thought showed Don in the truest light. It had character, and Don felt he had character too, and his car acted as a kind of real life dike between him and the men with beards and sweaters. Taking the Saab on a seventeen-hour road trip through very long patches of nothingness was a real act of courage and a sign that he was not simply another man on a committee that Leanne could make help out with K-P duty or children's story hour. B. There was another reason Don wanted to drive, and this reason was darker than lone-wolf bravado. It seemed as of late Don had been experiencing a sound and scent problem with Leanne when they were intimate, and while at first it was simply uncomfortable, it had now become nearly unbearable. Don hoped that perhaps a long drive towards the middle would clear up or somehow shine some light on the situation and how he might go forward with it or possibly even find a solution to the problem. You see, lately when he and Leanne commenced lovemaking, a frightening hypersensitivity to sounds and smells had arisen, making it nearly impossible for him to press near her, let alone climax. Entering her now emitted this sound like a large metal spoon entering a large bowl of macaroni salad. And her breathing was a little blocked as if she had to blow her nose (and asking her if she could please go blow her nose, Don learned, was not a good thing to do). And there were these pained little grunts—not deep moans of pleasure—but little grunts indicating bodily fatigue. Then there were the smells. Leanne, though relatively fastidious concerning her grooming, had as of late emitted a kind of soup smell that seemed to emanate from both her speaking and nether mouths. It wasn't awful soup, but still, it was onions and cabbage and carrots and turnips and leeks and longtime cooking. Also, her skin had taken on a pond-like smell, and it was difficult to remember she was a girl when he smelled her neck. The only thing that was keeping Don together was Leanne's last remaining oasis: her hair. Somehow, her hair had not come under curse and was still a wondrously soft pile of butter-colored curls that smelled just like sun and soap. So, you see, Don had some really good reasons to choose to drive to Indiana instead of taking the offered flight.

Don left for Lafayette, Indiana at five in the morning and, much to his pride, made it there in just under seventeen hours. The hotel, blocks from the University, was decorated in a kind of faux historical manner and was bustling with other scholars from all over. It was late in the evening when he arrived, so after a few beers and a complimentary hot dog at the bar, Don turned in, happy to be alone and well in Indiana. The first day of meetings felt less like an interview and more like a visit, as most of the day was him being shown the campus and introduced to many, if not most, of the faculty, graduate students, and staff. There was a freshness, an openness to Purdue's campus that was not present at Cornell or Stanford. Don wondered if he and Leanne could be happy in this type of environment. So many years were spent pushing against the pressure of intense self-importance that he wondered if he would unravel in the presence of so much niceness. Lafayette and West Lafayette and Purdue and Indiana were all just glowing with niceness. At the end of the day, aching with hellos and demure showmanship, the head of the department had invited Don to a barbecue back at his small farm just twenty minutes out of town. Don, of course, accepted the invitation.

The head of the department's small farm was not as small as Don had expected, and his home was far more opulent and his wife far more elegant than he had imagined would be. And very quickly, Don realized he had jumped to way too many assumptions regarding Indiana, the middle, and its people. This niceness, openness, and politeness were still present, but it had a blinding quality that could lead one to chronically underestimate the people being so nice and polite. And throughout the night, a pesky, terrible idea kept buzzing Don's ears as he drifted between pods of handsome, kind, open people: if it seemed that Don had keenly underestimated the accomplishments and dominion of these Purdue professors and local professionals, was it possible that he indeed had been over-estimating both himself and so many others throughout his career that were in no way nice, open, or polite?

Luckily, this was only a slight buzz for what was really bothering Don, or rather torturing Don, was his host's next door neighbor Becca. Becca owned a horse stable and small cattle operation called the Lazy S Ranch and was a little older than him and was possibly the most beautiful and alluring woman he had ever met in person. In her youth, she had been a fashion model, and by the way the hostess teased her (for they were close friends), Don sensed that she had been a model of some renown. The ranch came out of a previous marriage, and instead of returning to a life of dress-up and urbanity, Becca had chosen to continue her solitude in the prairie. However, it was clear that the prairie had not chosen her, as she still appeared wildly out of place. When talking to her close up or staring at her from a distance, she appeared more like an aberration than a person who lived next door and easily—naturally strolled over for some barbecue and conviviality. It was as if the prairie was for her a strange way station, and she was waiting with a ticket in hand. Waiting—that was what Don realized what made her so unbelievably attractive—she had the same cloud of dream around her that beautiful women do when they are waiting. Now, Don had never had the opportunity to sit down with or get to know these gorgeous waiting phantoms, but he had seen them all of his life.

As the night grew and the guests thinned, Becca gently announced she was leaving, at which point the hostess then insisted that her husband, the host, walk her back to her property, for while they were indeed next door neighbors, there was still some distance between the two doors. Don, looking over and seeing his potential new boss pouring another layer of salt and ice on one of the several ice-cream makers, blurted out to a warm and innocent pod of women that he would walk Becca home. He continued on, saying that he really loved horses and wanted to see the ranch and that the host looked pretty occupied with ice cream making. "Thank you," said Becca. And off they went. Into the prairie. In the dark night. For these things do evolve very naturally under stars.

Now, there are all kinds of seductions, and while I am tempted to spend a lot of time with all kinds of nuance and gingerly and perhaps a little of Beethoven's Symphony No. 9 (which is tempting, because I am, in fact, listening to it right now), in truth, Don and Becca began to fall in one of the most normal ways I know. They drank a great deal of very good wine and found that they had a great deal in common particularly in the things they did not have in common. She had a profound faith in God and ghosts and he in man and science. She preferred without apology art over the natural, and he not only felt his only peace in nature, but mistrusted absolutely everything that did not have a purpose. She did have a son and loved him plainly but felt fine with her husband taking primary custody while he and Leanne obsessed with every turn imaginable concerning their twins. So between the gapless conversation, the distinct smell of horse stables, and a few bottles of Burgundy white (which of course, Don did not admit to never having before), they fell into the fire nearly automatically.

Don was no virgin, and there had been others before he met his wife Leanne, but there was nothing that could have ever prepared the poor gent for a woman like Becca.

Her taste, the vacuum commenced with her taste. Both her speaking mouth and nether mouth tasted just like the rivers in Montana he grew up fishing in. But it wasn't just the smell and taste of the river water, but particularly in the case of her nether mouth, it was the sun-dried river stones that he would suck on as a child. The river rocks were warm and smooth and tasted softly of salt and mineral. He loved that taste and had all but forgotten that taste until he tasted her. And with every deep tasting, the Montana rivers and his youth grew brighter and brighter, and for a moment, he was the river and the sun and the smooth dried river rock and the salt and the mineral, and when Becca would move, it had the noble force of water and gravity against rock. The blissful memory and the blissful present were growing to such an aching perfection, Don felt as if the only possible way he could find relief was if he outright climbed into her. There was this one moment when she had enveloped one of his legs between her thighs, and she was kissing his chest as if nursing him, and somehow with a most gentle and most potent rhythmic press of her torso, Don felt as if his whole body was his sex organ, and his whole body enjoyed the painful pleasure-pull of entry and exit. The effect was so intense and so complete if you were to ask Don where his *part* was or her *part* was, he would not know because, in truth, they had become a singular swollen nerve (something Don had never heard or read could happen). This rushing oneness broke his dike of being to such a point that he realized (and only because there was so much salt and mineral-laced water) that tears were running down his face, causing a taste and scent between the two that could rival youth or gasoline.

"I will drive you back to your car," she said.

Don was so sad to go that he resented every piece of clothing on his and her body, and he almost hated her, because he had to leave her. In truth, that kind of sex is so close to death that one really should not go looking for it. However, in Don's case, he did not have any choice. And I suppose, just like death, if this kind of sex does happen to you, most likely you would not have had any choice either. (Blame Chuang Chou!)

"Did you hear that?" asked Don as her truck stopped next to his now rain glazed Saab.

"Hear what?" she asked.

"It's weird; I thought I heard someone reading," he returned.

"It is late," she said.

Don could not get out of her truck, and she sensed that. "One more bite. One needs to have two bites to taste something," she said warmly.

"What do you mean?" asked Don.

"Well, it is a little embarrassing, but I have a diet book that plainly explains why French women are thinner than American women. One of her theories is that French women only need two bites to truly taste something, and that once they have truly tasted something, they feel completely fine with pushing the plate away. It seems fat American women just eat and eat, forgetting that one only needs two bites to truly taste something. So, perhaps we should treat us like a French woman would her dinner?"

Don felt as if he could nearly faint from happiness, for he was lightly shaking. This was the solution, one more bite, and all will be well. He could return to Leanne in peace as well as leave Becca in peace. In the kind of peace that can only be had if one knew that they had truly absolutely tasted it. "Tonight?" asked Don.

"Late, for there are neighbors," she answered.

Don climbed in his beloved car with a feeling that could only be described as *Royal*. And then, and then that reading sound happened, but this time it was clearer, and he knew the voice. It was Leanne's voice. Don's hand shook out of a Poe-like, chilly sense that perhaps he had forgotten too many things when making his estimations. The key in his hand was barely held steady as he worked it into its slot. Again he heard reading, and it was clear, and it was Leanne. Don's heart pounded, and an intense roar of nausea jolted him. "This must be guilt," he thought. Don then turned the key, and along with the familiar coughing start of his car, a painfully blinding blanket of light fell over his face.

Don started to blink his eyes rapidly, and he felt alarmingly horizontal as if he were lying down. He let out an involuntary moan. The bright light was still cruelly pungent.

"Don, Don, can you hear me?"

Don looked up, and his wife Leanne with a very wretched face was hovering over him.

"Where am I?" asked Don.

"Ithaca, Don, you're in Ithaca," said Leanne while crying. "You were in a very bad accident just out of town on Highway 17. You have been in a coma. I've been reading to you, Don. They said you might be able to hear me. Oh, Don, I'm so happy you are awake."

He never did have her. It is bad enough to miss something that you had, but to miss something that you thought you had only to realize that you indeed did not ever have was truly brutal. *He never did have her.*

Don realized over and over throughout the duration of his life that it did matter if something was real or not. For truly sex with Becca had ever altered his sense of being and *being with*. He would never find the oneness or the becoming a river again, and it seemed that no matter how hard he tried to find that bliss, the real simply could not provide the experience, and because his time with Becca was not real, he was never able to comfort himself with the palliative of possibility. So, poor Don was left with the most incredible experience of his life that may or may not ever be possible, for if his singular bite of heaven had *really* happened, there was always the potential it could be tasted again. Without the anchor of the real, his bite of heaven was as solid and provable and repeatable (something scientists state their art on) as any god or ghost.

I am tired now (or rather I want to return to the real with its fun and music and kitchens) and no longer upset with the virtual or real Dons of the World. And my fictional tale is done. I suppose I need to land this thing before I start drifting into ever more murky waters regarding science, technology, and society. I will say that most likely we will be strapping all sorts of people (including happy to be strapped three-year-olds) into gizmos that fool our brains into thinking we have done things that we actually did not do. However, if there is a possibility of harm, then we really should poke at it repeatedly and ask things like "what if" and "how do you know" and "long term effects" and "usage parameters." For I do not believe inevitability should relieve us from the burden of morality.

Lastly, why all the jibber jabber about fiction

this and real life that, and why throughout this whole rambling thing do I keep interrupting the story and bring up my boring, real life? It is simply to show that the virtual reality found in fiction is indeed fed and made lush by the real. (Even if that real is actually pretty dull.) Consequently, if we as a society continue to not only pursue but to *prefer* virtual reality over the (crumby old) real, then soon enough, that sexy, swollen virtual reality will grow ever more anemic until finally withered. We will need artists to create our virtual realities, and artists need the real in order to create. If even our artists and writers lose the ground of the real, we are all in for some pretty lame experiences. Look, I love to make up stories and have all sorts of wonderful and terrible things happen to people I see on television, but I also know (or at least try to keep knowing) that all the meat and wine is to be found here, now, in the real.

How They Approach Landing (Annabel)

Annabel exhausted people, but she made it feel better than they thought exhaustion could. Annabel had girdled her husband with fear, but the clawing fear she wrapped him with was peculiar in that it suckled sweetly too.

She looked so much like a line of crows bursting out of a summer's thunderclap cloud that facing her for the first time would almost make you flinch. Holding her was to say goodbye to all and any sensible futures. Hard-worked, sunny plans fractured when men put their hands on the back of Annabel's head. Everything flew and struck when they did, when they tried. Her mouth, arms, legs, and heartbeat spread broadly like unnaturally dark wings and shimmered like hard, tiny-sharp rain. Her hair was liquid jet black and would only wave if she was sleepless and unshowered; her skin was greenish, pure white without a flaw or pore or slack; her smile was shockingly wide in reddish purple lips, and her teeth and gums almost glowed a little blue, as she was often cold for lack of eating or blood pressure; her body was a drape of milk with a velvety thumbprint patch of jet black crowning wide set, gapped legs and two tiny, dark brown pucker-nibble-pressing nipples; her skeleton looked like animated cursive as she moved with clothes or without, as she was slim with just enough flesh to manage arcs and rare showings of round; she dressed like she only used her sense of touch; she stood five-foot-four.

She never wore makeup or perfume nor did she do more than wash, clip, brush, and file. She had two eyes. They were large and almond shaped. One of the eyes was the color of the flesh of a lime: the whitest and yellowest green can be before it becomes something else. That eye, the pale, golden green eye, was outlined with a thin, inky line of purple brown blue. The other eye was translucent, dark brown. Her eyes always looked sad even when she was laughing or happy; it did not matter. She had elephant eyelashes that were naturally tar black. They were incredibly long, spirited, and somber just like an elephant's eyelashes. Annabel was what could best be categorized as a functional anorexic, as she was really never going to die from it, not directly at least.

Annabel could sit with profound patience. She willfully waited out miles without much thought or unease. She knew how to fade—how to go numb within and become a passenger. It was a conscious skill of hers; she knew she had this talent; it gave her a frightening degree of reckless courage. She could be torn apart by lions and remain as inert and indurate as a mattress. Stenography school was notorious for rampant dropping-out, as the tedium became nearly unbearable for most. For Annabel, it was a godsend, a dream opportunity to earn a living invisibly, silently as a blood and bone stuffed chair. She hated feeling; she hated talking to people; she hated eating.

However, Annabel did love a few things in life. She loved drugs. She loved expensive things. She loved sex. Drugs, expensive things, and sex for a girl with elephant eyelashes, non-lethal anorexia, and snow pale skin drew in all kinds of earnest, romantic, terrible boys and men and slow motion bouts of toss tumble torn. But she was married. She was caught and carried by a young man who was then twenty-nine and she twenty-four. Marriage had saved her life but had not fostered or provided a life that Annabel felt compelled to live and thrive.

May's splayed-hand, green leaves waved above the dirty, pitted streets of East Cambridge. The trees and their promised-delivered, eye-easing leaves were an assertion that God was everywhere. Annabel was an assertion of the omnipresence of human needy want. Not only God but Annabel knew these intricate, skinny streets well.

The tall, phoenix-leaved trees blurred along

through the sunroof of Annabel's black Honda Civic. Annabel's car floated through East Cambridge awesomely at home just like a housecoat or limp-swagger resident. There was a breeze too. It was just lightly cool and warm. It was the second of May, and early May had these kinds of mixed sensual breezes. When Annabel's black, liquidy hair flew against her bare cheeks and bare shoulders and sometimes had to be pulled from her bare mouth, her nerves would almost fall in love with being. She was always so pitter-patter happy when she was completely, unremorsefully committed to a drug run. She had had to make do with alcohol, cigarettes, and her neighbor's bad, always stale pot for the past (brutal and under-pressure sworn) two months, as a barely brush with an overdose had caused all sorts of insincere promises to her husband that she was off drugs for good. She could be loose with him regarding her promises, as they had had this exchange several times both in their courtship and ensuing marriage. In reality, Annabel had a good point in never feeling guilty on going back on her promises to quit—her addiction was, after all, the most honest thing about her. How could he love her without it if he claimed he loved her? She was a little right on this (which is not common in addicts' lines of rationale); her husband, though not consciously, had a heart that thrived on other's ruin.

Annabel reached her cousin's boyfriend's house. It was a large, two level duplex split down the middle. The house was built in the early twentieth century (like most of the shanty leaning, dead mouse smelling neighborhood) and was painted a sickly apricot color with rusty blood trim. The tree in front of the house was large and was tearing up the concrete that surrounded it. Several cigarette butts, spent lotto tickets, and faded wrappers of this and that fallen forgotten ringed the tree. A handful of young men were smoking cigarettes in front of their expensive, imported cars which were almost piled up on the street and faded asphalt driveway on the side of the house. The men were not in a huddle, rather, they were in a line. There were fair Irish arms. As Annabel pulled up and parked across from the pale-blue-eyed thug line, her brown and lime eyes ran down all of the young men's pale, fine formed though ugly formed too (in all the bad things they did) arms. Their arms all seemed to shine and flex and bully and beg as she walked towards them. Some had tattoos, but they were not big or overdone; the young men really were still young men, and there was not yet enough memory in the dumbly swaggering boys to really need large tattoos yet. However, as young and naively brave these boy's hearts and eyes and side-clippered heads were, their arms had something—a kind of mess of lock-hold and silky that made Annabel feel the warm, May air on her eyelids more than usual, as the quick thought of touching them with the tip of her tongue or gripping them nearly to the point of bloodletting made her naked lids lightly puff up.

Annabel's cousin Nicky ran out of the back door

of the first duplex in line and met Annabel in front of the car-packed driveway. She was nervous. She had been nervous since Annabel texted her and told her she was coming over. Her mother was Annabel's mother's sister, and Nicky's mother had been rough and sloppy with her life. Annabel's mother was hard and smooth and had taken in her sister's daughter and son many times. Both of the cousins' mothers were divorced, devoutly single, and bitter in their worship. The two cousins could not have been more different. Nicky was fairly tall at five-foot-seven and had chestnut-colored hair that she dyed light blond. Her skin was freckled and almost always a ruddy tan color. She smiled brightly and cried and screamed. She had large round breasts that were always toppling out of her tank top and firm, though round and full, thighs and buttocks. Boys loved her; her Irish, budding criminal boyfriend liked her a great deal. However, she did not have what her cousin Annabel did when it came to boys. Boys and men did not like Annabel, rather, they wanted to open Annabel up. When a man gets it in his head that he wants to open a girl up, his life becomes a kind of waiting game that grows increasingly desperate as failure progresses. As the routine becomes tighter and tighter, like the cranking down of a bolt, the man or boy gets to the point that they would nearly die for a peep and a hooked touch. And that *nearly die for* was a precious thing for any man in a cold numb world. Nicky was young (she was twenty-three—six years Annabel's junior), but she was old too (being raised by a rough and sloppy woman), and she knew all of this about her cousin Annabel and just how dangerous it made Annabel. So, she had curled under the front window on the second floor of the duplex in her and her boyfriend's bedroom and looked out for Annabel. Her plan was to get to her cousin Annabel before her boyfriend did and to make the deal instead of her boyfriend. Nicky was too late though.

Nicky ran to her cousin barefoot, tan, with a tiny tank top revealing large, tan breasts and a tiny pair of denim cut-offs for which you could easily see the multiple, grape-sized bruises on her inner thighs. Annabel was standing underneath the bent, closely clippered head of her boyfriend. His translucent blond hair glittered, as though polished, in the bright, diamond-clear sun. He was beguiled. Nicky began to slightly shake.

"Baby, here's some money. Go get us some beers and something to eat. I'm starving. You hungry?" Nicky's boyfriend, Tommy, asked Annabel. "No," he quickly rejoined, "you look like those girls who don't eat nothing." Tommy then handed Nicky a thick fold of bills without convincingly looking at her.

"Hey Annabel," softly, sadly said Nicky.

"Hey Nicky," returned Annabel.

"What do you want?" asked Nicky, trying to lengthen or change the moment between her and her boyfriend.

"I don't care," laughed Tommy, "just pick what you want."

"But what do you want," whined Nicky.

"I said I don't fucking care!" returned Tommy. He shouted at her, fully facing her with his body arched towards her and both of his arms out as though he were simultaneously blessing her and threatening her.

"Mikey, you better fucking go with me!" yelled Nicky, "I'm going to need somebody to help me with all the fucking shit."

A muscular nineteen-year-old man peeled off the line of thugs and obediently followed Nicky to her car.

"And no fucking Chinese or any Thai shit or any of that Asian crap this time, Nicky! I puke when I smell that shit!" yelled Tommy out to Nicky as she pulled away.

"Let's go upstairs," said Tommy to Annabel.

Tommy lit a small pipe and took a long hit. He then handed it to Annabel. Annabel took the pot-filled pipe and toked on it instinctively, and yet, there were faint notes of mania too as her body swayed not rightly, and her eyes touched upon things a little too hard, a little too clumsily. Tommy then chopped lines of Ritalin on top of a tidy, though cluttered, mirror-topped dresser that was antique and surprisingly of good quality. It was not a rare piece of furniture nor was it worth a great deal of money. However, it was on its own handsome and well made. It had a sense of use and worth and solidity that betrayed the chest-hollow energy between Tommy and Annabel. The energy of Tommy and Annabel was not black or sluggish nor was it dark or evil. It was hollow, void, and yet jittery and prickly too. It was close to ether or the last conscious seconds of sodium pentothal. There was a smell too; it was barely of oranges and mold and man.

After the lines, they split a beer and spent the night together for a half of an hour. While they embraced, Annabel took note of all the contents of Tommy and her cousin's bedroom without judgment, curiosity, or care as though she were simply cataloguing the contents of an estate. The walls were painted a chalky blue that often is seen on plastic balls and plastic toys for toddlers; it was almost the blue of the French flag though lighter and less good. A rosary hung above the bed. It was hung on a small yellow thumbtack. There was a white, rectangular plastic basket of folded clothes underneath the window looking out to the street. Several pairs of her cousin's satin underwear were on top. She could see jeans and flannel shirts poking through the holes of the basket. But the grime of salty high and impersonal, nearly hurting sex lorded over all that she saw. She almost wanted to chew something—like a bedsheet or an arm—so she could press even harder against her near-nausea-need and her loaded nerves. There was only sensation; there was no personality or care or consideration or obligation or promise; she would have been completely fine with being killed in that half of an hour.

She stood up and instantly appeared dressed;

she did; it was phantom-like. Tommy grabbed her more swiftly than she deemed he could or more importantly, would have wanted to. "Come'ere," he said with a dumb grin. He was very young; he was only twenty. "Come'ere," he repeated as he held her against his chest. Annabel stayed in his grasp coldly. Annabel was not good to grab. At first the grabber might feel strong, triumphant, but soon it becomes clear to the grabber that they had very little in their arms after all. It was a haunting effect, and even the young drug dealer shuddered a bit before reflexively returning her to standing. Annabel knew not only how to make her body eerily small and slight, she also knew how to shrink and fade her soul and presence.

Annabel took her small bag of amber-colored opium flakes, a small bag of pot, and a white envelope with a dozen Ritalin pills and put them in her small black purse. It was a dainty, ladylike purse. Tommy had admired it but did not want to tell Annabel that he liked it. In fact, he almost felt angry when he found himself liking her small, fine, ladylike, leather handbag. She then pulled out some bills and handed them to Tommy.

"Put the money on the dresser. I don't like girls handing me money," he said.

Nicky had not yet returned when Annabel headed towards Boston where she and her husband Jakob lived in the Back Bay.

The door to their apartment was painted red. It was carefully painted; the red looked almost like patent leather; the Ritalin had swelled her. She felt compelled to touch the slick red door and did touch it lightly. There was a handsome, brass number eight on their apartment door. They lived on Commonwealth Avenue in the Back Bay neighborhood just a few blocks from the Boston Commons. The entire living room was held fast with an enormous multi-paned bay window. The top panes were small, leaded glass; the May light became diamond as it sliced patterns into the creamy golden wooden floors and beige leather furniture. A large palm became a million pieces of emerald in the corner; Annabel stared at it as she put a large amber gem on top of a small mossy pinch of marijuana and lit her pipe.

Oh god floating heaven. Annabel wanted the whole world to screw her. She put on some music and swayed to the kitchen and poured herself a glass of red wine from an open bottle on the counter. Their kitchen was a small galley kitchen that opened up to the living room with a small side area that held a small dining table for four (six with slight effort). It was impeccable in every way, including high-end appliances and a packed wine cooler above the fridge that always required Annabel to stand on a chair. Annabel loosely sipped on her wine. The lines of Ritalin were making her wildly aroused. The opium was making her nearly air. The wine tasted like wealth, like blood, like a cut that burned just a little. She sat on the floor and then stretched out onto her stomach. She arched up her body like a cat and returned her pelvis again to the floor. Her mind was the light and the music and her sex. But she was not mind or body or light or sex. She flickered back and forth between being and not being. A memory would roll across, and then even her name became elusive. She changed the music and took off all of her clothes excepting for her tiny pair of pale, very pale, nearly dead, pink lace underwear that she spent ninety dollars on. They were so lovely. It was a perfectly pleasurable moment when she purchased them. The sales associate took endless care in folding them in tissue and packing them in a heavy, rope-handled bag. She ran her hands all over the delicate silk lace. The fineness—Annabel ached with want of more lace and more preciously wrapped things.

The electricity and the syrupy heat of opium and Ritalin was driving other lusts too; she dreamed of ghosts running between her legs and out of her mouth. She wanted to beg. She arose and stood, wearing only her pink lace underwear, in front of the second-floor bay window and re-lit her pipe. Even her nipples sucked in the creamy smoke. Annabel felt perfectly delightfully desperate (she briefly thought of swallowing the pipe whole).

Annabel's waking consciousness disappeared. Her dream mind had taken over. People were getting out of work and walking their dogs and sitting on benches convivially at the time.

When she reappeared, she was in the handsome apartment's only bedroom. Her heart was racing as her legs hung wide apart over the end of the fine linen dressed bed. She stood up unexpectedly and ran to the kitchen to pour another glass of wine, and snorted another line of Ritalin. Holding her glass of wine, she walked around her apartment like a delicate fair deer on a forest trail—not really in circles but in a pattern nonetheless. Nothing she could do felt wide enough.

The light was gone, and the large, multi-paned bay window that held the entire living room now appeared like a spider's head with several shiny black eyes. Annabel grimaced at the coldness of them. She then lowered the off-white Roman shades and proceeded to turn on every light in the apartment, including the pull-chain light in the coat closet in the hall that was used by her husband as a clothes closet. His closet smelled lightly of his cologne. Annabel sunk into Indian style in front of the open hallway closet and picked up his shoes to smell the insides. They all had a pleasant, extravagant leather body odor to them. She briefly sucked on one pair's laces and then spritely sprang up to change the music and grab a cigarette to have on their bedroom's tiny, narrow balcony (it held just two antique wooden dining room chairs). Before stepping out onto the balcony, Annabel slipped on a long, gray-knit tank dress that brushed the tops of her feet. The skin-tight dress made her appear almost naked, as her primarily bone presence gave off precise lines like a map.

She happily smoked as fresh-looking young people walked towards Newbury Street and finely suited gentlemen and ladies with wan faces and looser order headed towards the Charles River. Cars were still impatient; it was still time to go home and not yet fully into escape hours. Her day had been slow with only two depositions and a couple hours' worth of transcribing that was due early the next morning. She had a full day; however, tomorrow (which did not stress her at the moment, as excepting for extreme sexual arousal, she felt nothing really) would be packed. One of her depositions that day had been of a man who claimed he killed his wife in self-defense. He was still being held at the county jailhouse. This seemed unusual to her, and she almost had the mind to ponder why he was still being held, but then a cab slammed into a screeching halt at the corner stop sign, and she lost her entire train of thought. The event made her jump. She then removed herself from the balcony and carefully, almost like an examining doctor, closed and locked the small, glass, French doors.

There was a light thought, or perhaps it would be better described as memory, of her husband coming home and setting down his briefcase on the kitchen table and pouring himself a glass of scotch and saying things and walking around with heavy soled shoes looking for her. It was, for a time in their marriage, a ritual so repeated Annabel had become to see it as thoughtlessly as she saw the moon or the morning. Tonight, her husband was not coming home—was not going to share his day over making dinner or watching the news on the television. While she was on the balcony, he had texted her and told her he was working late. He had been working late or out of town every night since he found her nearly dead from a fentanyl overdose. There was a steep drop in mood as she felt a strange and heavy blanket of fear and abandonment. Luckily, the drugs were still quite strong, and this blanket fell away as the Ritalin drove thoughts and time speedily forward, and the amnesiac opium quickly swept away any and all accidents on the highway. She then pulled her dress off over her head while looking at herself in a free-standing, full-length mirror. It was time to take a shower. As she entered the pristine, white tiled shower, she briefly thought about how much it felt like a punishment to eat and then quickly shuddered that she had the thought.

Jakob Stuart Fordham was thirty-four years old—five years his wife's senior. He was blond, and his skin was smooth and lightly tanned. He was safely tall at six-foot-two inches and had a stout, athletic build (with just the tiniest, teeniest gesture of corporal indulgence). He played lacrosse in high school though not in college. However, he always felt in college that if he were to have only applied himself, he could have made the team. Jakob, known mainly as Jake, commonly saw unachieved things as awesomely achievable—achievable if only he were to apply himself a bit more aggressively. However, he never walked his thoughts out far enough to question why he did not then apply himself more aggressively. Instead, he simply carried a weak sense of bewilderment and possibly injustice as to why he was not quite as successful as his peers who already had children and owned houses and had too much money for ordinary banks and needed firms and funds for the excess. He was, though, superior in grooming and dress—something he and his wife, Annabel, had in common. Both were equally eerily scrubbed, pressed and scuff-free; as a pair, they drew many eyes and much attention and were not only consciously aware but also were pleased by the fact.

Jakob attended Hobart College in Geneva, NY where he majored in business administration. He graduated with a respectable 3.1 grade average (which could have at least been a 3.8 if he had drank less beer and studied more) and moved to Boston immediately after school where he took a position selling software for a firm in Cambridge, MA.

Jakob met Annabel in Cambridge at a bar in Harvard Square. She was twenty-one and was celebrating passing her stenography exam. Jakob always liked weird, terrible women, and Annabel certainly topped all of his previous adventures with weird, terrible women. After only speaking to him for a half of an hour, she asked if he had a car; he said he had a car. She then asked if he had it with him. He said no. She was visibly disappointed. He asked her if she needed a ride. She said no but that she wanted to smoke some heroin. Jake was stunned. He had never met a person who actually did heroin. And she was so lovely and alive—it was completely the opposite of what kind of person Jake thought smoked heroin. "I do not live far from here...just over the bridge in Back Bay," Jake offered. "Let's go then," she said. Back at his tiny studio apartment on Marlborough Street, Annabel and he got very high. He was hooked; not on heroin, as the shame of doing something so dangerous prevented him from doing it ever again; he was hooked on Annabel, as she was the black hole he had been unconsciously seeking his whole life. He would always—no matter what—be better than her. But it was just a little more than that—a little more than simply finding a background that would make him appear taller—it was also a way for him to move steadily ahead through life.

The Fordhams were a willfully hemmed-in family. They took pride in constraint and mediocrity. Shouting, laughing, beating, risking, and most of all, making mistakes were considered abominations in Jakob's family, and while this type of upbringing did provide endless amounts of friends (to all members of the Fordham clan—they were all immensely socially popular) and solid material comfort (they were just wealthy enough to be tasteful, comfortable, and tony), it did mean a kind of willful interior entropy, a kind of cheery, march through it but don't fight it if you might not win malaise to pass as flesh and blood for the Fordham family. Marrying Annabel was marrying panic. She was a human battlefield. Jakob, of course, certainly could never take the risk to make a mistake, but Annabel did all sorts of risky, stupid things (and yet oddly, he never made the connection that in marrying Annabel he was taking an incredibly stupid risk). Each time she did fall hard without bracing (for she had as little brace as he had as much), he felt a python-like surge of life in his body. He felt almost as though he was making progress somehow as a man, as a human, each time Annabel messed up. She provided an intense, internal squeeze that pushed him forward in life. Without her, he felt (though none of this was conscious) as though he would turn to stone, inert, moss covered. He did not (again, none of this was conscious), however, see that the creature this arrangement resembled most was the earthworm—movement coming in progressive squeezes—poor Jakob would have loved to have been a lion or perhaps even a good hunting dog.

When he made love to his wife, he often worried he would pound her to death, as it felt too good—a wild good that seemed to Jakob as terrifying in that he might not be able to put on the breaks if he let the wild good fully overtake him (and always Annabel could rise his body to seemingly insanity causing levels of aching pleasure) (it always amazed Jakob that such a slight human never weighing a hundred pounds could provide so much electric squeeze and icy shiver). Consequently, he rarely did make love to her—it was too much risk—it might end up somehow wrong or bad. He was relieved that a small promotion he received just after he and Annabel were married took him to many faraway places and for ever-increasing lengths of time.

All in all, his promotions had been slow in

coming—this was becoming more apparent as his co-workers were becoming younger than him—and while it irked him greatly, he simply could not get himself to take the risk and move to another software company (it was the same company he had joined just out of college). Life, however, does not always let someone stay in their idiosyncratic personality ruts. The truth was while Annabel had never drawn Jakob over to the dark shores of hard drugs, her love of very fine things from shoes to apartments to bed linens had indeed become his obsession as well. They were both in very heavy debt (actually, on the brink of bankruptcy), and they were both completely reticent to face it. Jakob loved nothing better than to stroll down Commonwealth Avenue towards the Boston Commons in a bespoke suit and impeccable shoes. He was a sight to behold; he was admired by people of all ages, both men and women, and of many classes. He would smile, say "good day," and feel nearly really hero lion hunting-dog. Something, however, would have to change, and this Jakob knew. And this did make Jakob heart-heavy.

There was one more thing besides facing near-bankruptcy that was making Jakob Stuart Fordham heart-heavy, and that was the fact that his marriage was fully falling apart. His love of long away travel, his need to keep personally caged, and his fear of fully letting himself go sexually had after five years of marriage created some real rips and frays. Annabel too had done her part: missing loads of work due to heavy drug use; spending enormous amounts of money on fine dinners (dinners she never actually ate); spending enormous amounts of money on clothes and drugs; being unable to completely reign in her anorexia, causing several expensive health crises; and finally, an ever-growing sexual appetite that presently was taking her to darker skies than usual. She was a crow. He was an earthworm. However, there was without question a tether of relationship and commonality between the two creatures that perhaps suggested a deeper bond, a more entangled connection that might not be so easy to sever.

Jake sat at his desk and sadly watched his co-workers leave the office. He now hated being in town. It was a time to make service calls and receive extra technical training for the software products his company sold. Those things felt completely beneath him, and increasingly, the bitter pinch of sitting with guys and gals just out of college, of not yet having an office or support staff, and of never taking part in strategy (of just being told the new this or that procedure and the newest company focus—without, of course, any of his input) was causing him to want to run, escape. And yet, Jakob Stuart Fordham was the last man on earth who would flee. Jake would, though, drag, stall, and put-off—those were perfectly sane, acceptable things to do.

The first thing he would do to avoid home (apart from being nearly the last guy to leave the sales office) was go to the gym. His company had a deal with MIT, and the employees were all able to join MIT's fitness club. There was indoor tennis, a full gym, a swimming pool, several classes from yoga to weight training, and during the summer, there was even sailing on the Charles River. He spent twenty minutes running on the treadmill and then a half hour or so lifting weights. Never did he feel too connected to any of it. He did like it though; Jake could enjoy things even if he was a little bored and disconnected. It was a kind of grace that he was not incredibly picky when it came to experiences. He could like almost anything he was doing just so long as it did not involve the risk of him making a mistake. He sailed on the Charles only once.

After his workout, he showered and returned to his fine navy suit. He texted his wife and told her that he would be working very late and not to stay up. It was a queasy thing for him to do, as he still feared that something might be direly wrong with Annabel, for it was just two months since he found her nearly dead from an overdose of the synthetic heroin fentanyl. The dealer had sold Annabel the drug as heroin, but it was not. It was fentanyl, which is much stronger than normal street-grade heroin. All of this was explained to him as Annabel passively fought for her life in the intensive care unit. The doctor was Jakob's age, and somehow that made the event hurt all the more. Jakob kept on envisioning the doctor going home to his large, lovely house with a kind, loving wife who was a kind, loving mother to their bright and beautiful children. He kept on creating a story where the doctor would tell his sad, sympathetic wife about the young, decent-looking couple that somehow got involved with the devil, with street drugs. Simply texting Annabel and not calling (which at least was a way to see if she was okay) made Jakob feel shameful. However, it was all he could do; he was just so exhausted from fearing for her. He was just so exhausted with feeling shameful, both for his cowardice and her carelessness. He just could not bear to ever find Annabel like that again. So much so that he knew if he sensed she was like that again, he would never ever return home. This last inner conviction of Jakob's was not, however, real. He was afraid, and he was truly exhausted with Annabel, but he was not as cold or fatalistic as he imagined he was. He was just afraid. He was just exhausted.

It was almost completely dark out. Everyone was out. It was the second of May. The East Coast hibernators were ready to walk around outside at night with ease. No near-death slides on icy sidewalks or painful, burning, frost bitten faces sitting above stiff, heavy wool cocoons. He was happy to walk home. Even though it was dark, there were still some joggers on the sidewalk alongside the Charles River on Memorial Drive. He would enjoy the second when the girl joggers would pass him. He very often caught their eye; he was handsome; it was a pleasure for him to walk around. The girls almost always smiled right at him. The lights of Boston were perfectly mirrored in the water. It was a still, lovely night. His body felt wonderful from the work-out and shower. It only cramped up when he crossed Mass Ave. bridge and neared his and Annabel's apartment in the Back Bay. Jakob decided to pass Commonwealth Avenue where his place was and walk to Newbury Street. He then sat down at the bar of a loud and packed restaurant that was filled with very beautiful Bostonians and out-of-towners of all ages. There were large, five feet by five feet erotic paintings of men with women, men with men, and women with women lining the wood-paneled walls of the high-ceilinged restaurant. He and Annabel both loved to drink and dine there. He did not feel odd or ungentlemanly for not calling Annabel to join him. He increasingly put off going home. Seeing Annabel and the bills caused him to have to go completely numb, and Jake just wanted a little more of life animated before he went home.

"Are places always this packed in Boston?" asked a gentleman in his late fifties next to Jake.

"A lot of the time, but on the first genuinely warm night in May, everyone comes out," returned Jake. "My name is Jake Fordham. I'm in software sales." Jake then put out his hand. While Jake may have had many internal agonies regarding his place in life and the state of his financial and marital affairs, he was a Fordham and a salesman. He was never shy and was a genius at meeting people. Out of town strangers were his absolute favorite.

"Nice to meet you, Jake. I'm Chuck Spalding. I'm actually in real estate development back in Portland, Oregon. My daughter is here at Harvard, and I had a little business in Hartford consulting for an insurance company that is getting into insuring large construction projects, and so I thought I might as well swing by and pay my girl a visit...oh, and there she is...." The older gentleman turned towards a beautiful, small girl with very black and very shiny hair. Jake quickly assessed that he could not screw her. She appeared to be around nineteen. She was smiling and waving as she bumped and tapped-shouldered her way through the packed restaurant towards her father.

"Hi sweetie," said the man.

"Hi daddy," she answered.

An incredibly beautiful (though haunting and tired in the eyes) hostess quickly approached the father and daughter. She spoke with a dense, eastern European accent: "I see your daughter has arrived... we can seat you now." She sounded much older than she looked. Jakob made a note of her leaden beauty and fell a tiny bit in love. She wore dark blurred make-up around her eyes, and her long, dark blonde hair was pulled back in a low, smooth ponytail. Jakob noticed too that her black high heels revealed a touch of white plastic at the heel tips, showing hard wear. He thought of taking them off of her.

"Thank you much," convivially said the gentleman from Portland to the waiting hostess. The man then turned to a somewhat disappearing Jake, "Have a good night, you hear?"

"You too," Jake returned in an equally convivial tone. Jake could do convivial reflexively.

Jakob stood on the corner of Commonwealth and Exeter and stared up at his building. It was constructed of handsomely aged red brick, with the wood window framing and the wooden balconies painted a deep salmon color. The lights of their apartment were all on. He desperately wanted to see and to smell and to caress his wife, but his chest sunk too at the thought of getting the mail (Annabel never got the mail) and of perhaps finding Annabel nearly dead from an overdose like he did just a few months ago. The night air was cool and soft; Boston life was still roaring around—even where he stood. A small group of very drunk young women briefly surrounded him as they were trying to wave for a cab on the corner. He waved one for them. When one of the girls was sloppily sliding into the cab carelessly over her friends' legs and laps, her dress had slid up and revealed a nearly fully naked bottom with a paper sheath of a straw completely smoothly stuck on one of her cheeks. It was folded over and bent on the end, making an upside-down number seven. Jake became hard, as the sight was so completely unexpected and so completely erotic. She appeared so small and badly handled...he wanted to quickly reach in and grab her by the pelvis.

He chose not to get the mail. It could wait for the morning. He was still hyper aroused by the girl in the cab with the bare bottom. Now he was anxious to see Annabel. She was worse than any of those girls. She would have enough dark soil to completely bury him. He could be naked with her.

The girl from the cab, though, did still loom large as he climbed the stairs to the waiting red door number eight. He wondered briefly before he opened their apartment door what would have happened if he would have jumped in the cab with the girls. He thought of himself putting his hands all over her hips and thighs, perhaps under a table or in a dark corner. He then wondered briefly if he should enter the apartment at all. With a twinge of chore and hope, he opened the door.

The cab girl disappeared entirely from his memory forever when Jakob found Annabel. She was lying flat on her back on their living room floor. Traditional Japanese music was playing. The notes struck the ear as if the air and silence were potent drum skins. The flute moved around the sparse koto whines like a delicate, spontaneous stream. She was wearing a stunning, shell pink satin kimono embroidered with white chrysanthemums. Her eyes were wide open and nearly unbearably beautiful. The brown eye was sharp and brilliant and alert. The pale lime yellow white eye was drowning in transcendence. He stood over her. She swished her lightning and cloud eyes to his and smiled like a bird.

The Rafters
(Hera)

"Darling Zeus," began Hera, "What shall we do when this ends?" Hera was laying on the hot, smooth cement that encircled their Olympic-sized swimming pool. Her long hair cascaded around her oiled, tanned skin. Her thick, gold bracelets softly chimed as she sat up and dipped one of her toes in the pool. "This is going to end. I know it."

"Have you been reading more Buddhist works, my dear?" lovingly asked Zeus who was reading in a chaise-lounge just behind her.

I don't remember Gautama Buddha well," said Hera. She turned to her husband. He was wearing navy swim trunks and a buff-colored, short-sleeved linen shirt. His tanned skin, white beard, and hair glittered in the high sun. It was another stunning day on top of Mt. Olympus.

"That was during your intense child-rearing phase darling. As I recall, you were up to a birth a day...all you wanted to do then was cook, diaper, and get pregnant," jovially answered Zeus. He was deeply enjoying his wife's beauty. She was naked and still stunningly perfect in every way. She always was stunningly perfect in every way, and he always noticed it and always enjoyed it. Thousands and thousands of years had not even slightly dented neither his admiration nor the cause of it.

"Did you visit him? I mean after his enlightenment, did you join the heavenly host that regaled him while he sat under the Bodhi Tree in Bodh Gaya?" asked Hera.

"No, darling, I did not. As I recall, you had managed a pretty clever revenge against me. I believe I was trapped in the belly of a pretty hideous monster at the time. Brilliant move though...she really was convincing as a ravishing maid before she swallowed me whole and scared the wits out of me."

"You met with no harm," softly returned Hera.

Hera stood up. Zeus inhaled deeply and let out a soft, personal laugh, as she managed to make him almost nervous she excited him so much. "Going for a swim?" asked Zeus.

Hera with unimaginable grace climbed onto the diving board and dove into the pool. Hardly a sound was made. Her long, fine limbs cut through the water like young, slim dolphins. Her body made the water clap a sweet, sensual song. Zeus closed his eyes briefly and then thought to join her. As he rose, a mighty din rose as well. It began as a black prick in the center of the pool then rapidly grew into a great, black, cauldron-like opening. Six enormous sharks raced up into the pool and circled panicked Hera. Zeus transformed himself into a great eagle. He swooped over his wife and clutched her—flying her safely away from the attack. As they landed on the lawn that sloped down from their mansion, Hera, wet and weeping, clinched Zeus like a child. "It's almost time, Zeus. All things must go down—even us gods. It's almost time I finally meet death," she cried, "and I'm so afraid. What will I become? Have I been good? Have I been kind?"

That night at dinner, Hera could barely eat. Zeus tried all he could do to lighten her spirits. "I can feel it, Zeus. I tell you...death is near...and then Earth...or possibly worse. Zeus, what if I am made a ghost or a demon? According to Buddha, many gods go to hell upon their death...that we are too spoiled and too comfortable to think of things like enlightenment," moaned Hera sincerely as she ran her eyes over the cornucopia displayed before her. The meats and vegetables glowed and glinted so brightly that only Hera's very own beauty outshone them.

Zeus eyed his temperamental, jealous, powerful, and gorgeous wife thoughtfully and sighed. "Is that a new dress?" he asked, "It is simply lovely. I do not believe I have ever seen that shade of blue before... it is most intoxicating...I shall have a precious stone made in that very color, and I shall swallow one and place thousands of others deep inside the Earth's crust.

Hera's eyes rose to meet her husband's. A thick plate of tears glittered. "Really?" softly asked Hera.

"Truly," answered Zeus uncomfortably. There was a slight tremor in his voice. Hera was a lot of things, but being easily touched was not one of them. She was his sparring partner. His equal in every way. Nobody could be found that could test and sometimes best him in the Universe. And while he was happy to compliment and make glad Hera, he was not sure of the sensation of moving her.

After wiping a few tears from her flawless, tan face, Hera then unconsciously picked up a piece of bread and popped it in her mouth. Relieved, Zeus finally dove into his meal. Hera sat up as the servant filled her wine glass. Zeus then motioned for his glass to be filled. The servant stepped back into the shadows as the two rose their bejeweled chalices. A toast was made to Hera's blue (that Zeus was going to create a new precious stone after), and Hera threw in Buddha (much to Zeus' frustration), and as Zeus was about to sip a leaping cat drew his eyes to the side of the dining room, and there he saw her. The servant was not a servant, but Zeus' most recent and most scorned lover. The mistress had been most open with her murderous intent towards Hera after Zeus could no longer sincerely hide his profound love and passion for his wife. This was not uncommon, and it had never dawned on Zeus to feel worried by the threat, as Hera would have never let an attacker come this close in the past.

Zeus blanched as he saw Hera's cup touch her lips. "No, Hera!" he shouted.

Hera's body jumped out of surprise, and the chalice was dropped. The ex-lover bolted for the exit archway, Zeus foaming with rage, pushed the table onto its side and tackled his ex-lover, and he would have killed her on the spot—for he was strangling her—if Hera was not wailing with such tender and terrified despair.

He lifted his hands and person from the shocked murderess and clutched his wife. She was shaking and crying. "This is my last day, Zeus. This is my last day. I know it. I know it." She cried with such sadness and desperation that Zeus cried with her.

Zeus managed to calm his dear Hera and had convinced her that a long bath was what she needed. And while he was not convinced that death was going to take his wife that night, he did order several guards to stand sentry outside her bathing chamber.

Zeus wandered the rooms of his palace. Every chamber shone with complete dignity and opulence. Hera had built a fine home and a fine life for him. He could find a wondrous memory of his life with Hera in every room. Zeus laughed several times to himself, "It was so like Hera to manage a complete day of terror...and somehow my raw and shaken nerves only manage to love and think of her more." He then imagined her bathing while being convinced that she will die that night. This thought and image made his heart ache so much with love for Hera that he fled the house and entered the clear, black night.

"I love that damned goddess too much," he said to the empty sky. Zeus then made himself an owl and flew to Earth. He covered great portions of the night side. The trees smelled fine and the rivers even finer. "Am I to live here one day? As a human?" mused Zeus, "and would Hera remain with me?" And with that thought, his owl wings froze, and Zeus the bird tumbled to the ground. The pain of impact was tremendous. Zeus, still in owl form, stumbled to the side of a brook and climbed a large stone on the brook's bank.

The song of the brook was sweet and sensual. It reminded him of the sounds Hera made when she made love, as she always wore golden bracelets that would rhythmically drag on both of their bodies and clink against each other (and once against his teeth—which smarted greatly—but there was more laughter than pain after the fact). Then came the coldest squeeze of panic that the god had ever felt seize him. "Dear Hera, dear Hera," thought Zeus. Zeus flew as fast as the universe would allow back to Olympus. He was in such a panic—such a desperation—to assure himself that Hera was okay, he flew right into the mansion as an owl. It was only until he met with the guards at the bathing chamber door did he hastily return to his human-esque form. As his hand touched the door of the bath chamber, he felt so afraid that he briefly wished that he was dead.

"Zeus?" shrieked Hera who was having her

upper lip waxed. She was startled and deeply embarrassed. "Zeus, out!" she yelled with her hands over her face. "Out! I said," she repeated, but poor Zeus was so confused and emotionally overwhelmed that he could not move. "Zeus, please...you know you are not allowed in here," she said. Only this time she said it very lovingly and soft. "Oh Zeus, at least turn away for a moment."

Zeus at least could manage that. He turned his back to Hera. Hera motioned her cosmetician to finish, and the band of cotton was pulled. Heady tears dripped out of Hera's nose and the corners of her eyes. Hera then asked the other ladies-in-waiting to leave while patting her inflamed upper lip. "Now, don't forget to apply witch hazel on that," said her cosmetician as she left the bathing chamber.

"Yes, yes," hastily returned Hera.

"Otherwise it will blister," continued the cosmetician.

"Yes, yes, now please...leave us," exhaled Hera.

Zeus and Hera were left alone. He sat beside her on a small stool where the cosmetician had been seated. Hera was lying on a large, spotlit, adjustable chair. "Want to hand me the witch hazel?" asked Hera with feigned frustration.

"In the clear bottle?" asked Zeus.

"Yes, yes," returned Hera. It was clear she was still embarrassed by Zeus being there.

Zeus took the bottle and a handful of cotton balls. He hovered over her. "How bad does it hurt to have it done?" he asked, "because it looks pretty bad."

"Not as bad as this," she said as she lifted the white sheet that was draped over her and revealed a heavily inflamed bikini line with little patches of bruise and blood.

Zeus' eyes widened along with a soft, curiosity-drenched expression. He was also trying not to smile, as somehow it made him happy to see her this way. "I had no idea," he said.

Seeing Hera alive and fine and comical was making him want to laugh and cry and drink heavily and find a sweet maiden. "I was scared, Hera," quietly offered Zeus.

Hera sat up and wrapped the sheet around her powerful, glowing body. "I'm scared too," she quietly returned.

* * *

"Could you be any later?" whined Zeus' lover. "My hair is flat and so is my mood."

Zeus half-heartedly attempted to soothe his young nymph; however, he found himself already regretting leaving Hera. In truth, he took his nightly custom of sweet, sensual flight, because to change his behavior meant that perhaps Hera was truly in peril, and that for him was too much to bear.

His little nymph touched and curled her body round and round his continental strength. His chest and thighs and rare, rich arms could span the mass of the earth. And while this intoxicated the rosy, little churl, Zeus knew to his very core that Hera always grasped his hands and that only together could they hoist the heavens. They were one. Earth and water were convenient separations, but they were not the truth. The separation was intended to allow Zeus and Hera to explore existence, but in time, jealousy and delusion formed two of the most realistic illusions in the universe. And what gripped him—what caused him to almost dangerously throw his little nymph harshly off his body—was the instant recollection of Her as Him and Him as Her.

He decided to walk back to his palace. He had not walked home in thousands of years. His feet ached when he swung the heavy mansion doors open. He was so terribly sad and distraught by his horrible day and night that after he had entered his home, he did not bother to shut the gilded front doors.

His back felt the cool night air, and in one enormous moment, he felt mortality enter his house. The breeze of endings felt like ash or bits of dried leaves. The flutter did not burn, rather, it tickled. This confused Zeus. He was quite sure that a great turn of soil was heading towards the ground of his being; however, it spun and swayed and (this surprised him greatly)—it seemed close to even having a sense of humor.

Nonetheless, Zeus felt a sincere jump of panic when he felt a warm squeeze on his might mound of a shoulder. "Darling, it's just me," softly said Hera. "I was outside, and I saw you in the open doorway. It was such a sight, dear Zeus. I cannot remember seeing you in such a haunting and beautiful frame. It was as if the universe was allowing me one last stunning look."

Zeus turned to Hera. Unlike his nymphs, angels, and maidens, Hera was pure presence. Her face was sad, but her shoulders were strong enough to carry him. Her heart could glow through any feeling or action. Her face was swollen from agony, but there was a curl in Hera's expression that solved his love for her. Hera had a profound sense of humor, and it was Hera that was forcing the scythe to laugh and tickle. It was Hera that made misery and toil laugh too. And if Hera could bring death to lovely terms like the moon is lovely, like the sun is lovely, then his own stern self would blow delicate humor from leaden hell too.

"We're screwed, aren't we, dearest?" said Zeus with a young voice. It almost cracked.

Hera smiled ear to ear and laughed with such sincerity that whole stars poured out of her eyes. "Yes, darling, I believe we are."

Made in the USA
Middletown, DE
23 July 2017